Phoenix Quest

CARLA

LIFE IS AN ADVENTURE
ENJOY THE RIDE

JAMES

Phoenix Quest

The Medallions, The Ring and The Feather

James Malcolm

Copyright © 2011 by James Malcolm.

Library of Congress Control Number: 2011909015
ISBN: Hardcover   978-1-4628-8181-9
              Softcover   978-1-4628-8180-2
              Ebook   978-1-4628-8182-6

All rights reserved. No part of this book may be reproduced or transmitted in any form or by any means, electronic or mechanical, including photocopying, recording, or by any information storage and retrieval system, without permission in writing from the copyright owner.

This is a work of fiction. Names, characters, places and incidents either are the product of the author's imagination or are used fictitiously, and any resemblance to any actual persons, living or dead, events, or locales is entirely coincidental.

This book was printed in the United States of America.

To order additional copies of this book, contact:
Xlibris Corporation
1-888-795-4274
www.Xlibris.com
Orders@Xlibris.com

Contents

1. The Declaration 7
2. Revelations 24
3. Lorelei's Enchantment 40
4. Rhinegold Maidens 58
5. Edric's Magic 73
6. Nymphs, Seers, and Sirens 88
7. Spirits of the Sea 105
8. Twice Sail to Phaeacia 120
9. Intimidation of Lilith 136
10. Nefertiti's Gift 149
11. Two Feathers 163

Character Map 181

The Declaration

With a cool summer night breeze under an umbrella of stars, red-hot embers cast a dancing glow about the meager framework of Aiden's trade. His heavy hammer struck the glowing metal pressed against the anvil, with a rhythmic echo. Sweat rolled down the bulging muscles of his glistening torso. The blacksmith was a man of stature, unequaled by his peers.

It was the first time King Darian had requested his service since his father had passed on two years ago. The king, not easy to please, was reluctant to recognize the blacksmith's ability until now. His charge was a sword of detailed craftsmanship for Prince Gideon's sixteenth birthday, one week hence. Aiden was determined to surpass the doubting king's expectations, improving his standing within the realm as an honorable man in a dependable trade.

More importantly, there was the princess who'd caught his eye these many years. She was a vision of shoulder-length blonde hair, sensual blue eyes, and unmatched feminine beauty among the maidens of the realm, worthy of any man's heart and desire. He could only imagine such a union, unlikely as it might be, yet there were no royal prospects anywhere in the kingdoms to match her status. Ariana was the king's eldest daughter, in her late twenties, well-past the marriageable age, and as long as her standing remained unchanged, there was always a chance, no matter how small it seemed.

Aiden's integrity was without question. He was always to the point, from the heart, and honest to a fault. His character demanded respect in return, but not all appreciated his candor. To a small few, he was considered more of a threat and a rival. Aiden could be as hard on himself as Darian, particularly when maintaining his high self-imposed standards. He was by no means perfect, but sought perfection.

Sounds of hoof beats, pounding the clay, were approaching down the eastern road. It was late for travelers in a region with a history of rouges who'd rob unsuspecting wanderers under the cover of darkness. The blacksmith, armed with his sword, leaned against a wooden post, prepared for their arrival. Caution was a mandatory response, a key to survival, and a deterrent to those desperately aggressive souls who preyed on the weakness of others. As the three shadowed riders approached, Aiden had no fear, confident in his own ability, with a reputation of being sufficient with a blade.

As the silhouettes neared, it became obvious they were riders of means. Shields hung from the saddle horns, moonlight traced the lines of minimal armor, and the dress was more regal than drab. With a full beard and rugged stature, the king paced the trio forward. He was followed closely by a burgundy-hooded Ariana and Gideon stationed in the rear. The prince's long dark hair made him look older than his years and somewhat imposing in the saddle.

The blacksmith relaxed his stance, leaving the sword propped against the post. He stepped forward, greeting the three, ever-mindful of the princess. He was quick to catch Ariana's eye, holding the glance, until Darian became aware of their connection.

"How may I help you, sire?"

"I would hope your focus is not cause for concern on this late night. I've come to view the blade."

Aiden knew they hadn't ridden all this way simply to review his progress; the castle was in the opposite direction, and why would he bring the prince when it was his birthday gift?

"Sire, I do respect your request. I would rather delay your inspection until there is more to show if you please."

The king sat motionless in the saddle for several moments before casting a glance toward Gideon, then slowly back to the blacksmith, pausing briefly before gazing back at his daughter. Aiden could tell it was a serious stare, even before he became the king's target.

"Bring it to me in six days. I will judge at that time whether it be worthy or not. Don't disappoint, for it could impact your future."

"Yes, sire."

Aiden bowed his head, with a modest nod of acknowledgement and respect, while catching one last look of the princess. Darian jerked the reins suddenly, steering his horse to lead the others up the dark road. The blacksmith caught Ariana stealing a second glance as he watched them disappear into the shadows. Ariana was curious, that was sure, and the thought was more than enough to leave a smile on his face. Suddenly, seemingly out of nowhere, ten more well-armed riders galloped past. He couldn't help but wonder why the escort traveled at such a distance from the king.

Aiden, up with the sun, prepared oatmeal in the fire pot, knowing too well this would be a week of long days and late nights. While he ate, his thoughts drifted to the events of the night before. The rare, unexpected visit put a smile on his face once more. Confidently, he looked forward to delivering Gideon's sword and seeing the princess again.

The blacksmith grabbed a towel and stepped outside for his morning shower. Open to the elements, he pulled the rope attached to the overhead tank, releasing enough water to wet and lather with the lye bar. Going about his business, he was unaware there was company.

"Well, hello there and good morning. I hope I didn't catch you at a bad time."

"Depends on what you have in mind."

Aiden continued to lather, unbothered by her untimely interruption. He kept is focus on Scota, standing with her arms crossed and a confident grin enhancing her face. She was alone, carrying a twelve-inch ornamental dagger in a curved sheath strapped to her hip. She was interesting and attractive, not at all helpless as females go. She was somewhat of a mystery; about nineteen or twenty and few knew much about her.

"Strictly business, I'm sorry to say, except for the view."

"You're welcome to wait for me inside if you like."

"Would that make you feel more comfortable?"

"At this point, it really doesn't matter to me either way. There's nothing left for me to hide as you can plainly see."

"You're right, there's certainly nothing left for the imagination."

She smiled, slowly turning toward the front door of his abode. Aiden finished rinsing off the soap, dried, and then dressed, smirking over the well-timed encounter on her part. He hadn't seen Scota since the market, a couple months prior. Her people had built a settlement along the northern coast a little more than a year ago. None were native to the island, and rumors were they sailed a great distance to build here. She had never volunteered any information, and he never asked. He knew there was more to her story that remained hidden.

When Aiden opened the door, Scota was sitting at the table, enjoying a bowl of his oatmeal. He was pleased that she wasn't afraid to make herself comfortable.

"Business you say, do you need another horse?"

"No, it's something more delicate and personal. I have a piece of jewelry with a broken chain. I'm hoping you can repair it."

She reached into a bag tied around her sash and laid the necklace on the table. The medallion was a significant piece with the image of a bird unlike anything he'd ever seen before.

"Is this gold?"

"Yes, have you worked with gold before?"

"Twice, gold's not difficult to ply, it's only difficult to find."

"How long do you think it will take?"

"Maybe an hour, not much longer. I can repair it while you wait."

"That would be great."

"We don't see much gold on the island. I certainly wouldn't advertise by carrying it around, especially when you travel alone."

"I do keep it hidden, and nobody would want to face the point of my dagger."

"The necklace is high quality and very unusual. How did you come by it?"

"My mother gave it to me."

"Does the bird have significance?"

"The bird is a white vulture. It represents the goddess Mut, lady of heaven. She is the mother of the gods and the waters from which everything is born."

"No disrespect, but here, mutt is a dog without pedigree and why a vulture?"

"In Egypt, a white vulture is considered a maternal creature, and the queen is the high priestess of the temple."

"Where is Egypt?"

"On a distant shore of an inland sea, a long way from here."

"If you don't mind me asking, you smell sweet. I've noticed it before, but I haven't wanted to impose."

"It's saffron, used in medical treatments, perfume, and as an offering to the gods. And I don't mind your curiosity, remember, I've seen you naked, and I was reasonably comfortable with that."

"Well, I can't worry about things I can't control. Hopefully, you won't always see me that way."

"I'm sure the memory will be hard to erase, but I'll try my best."

"About as hard as I would if the roles were reversed. I see the medallion has orange stones around the edge."

"Carnelian, a gem from the isle of Crete."

"Crete?"

"Inland sea. There are many civilizations there, more advanced than we are here."

"Why would you ever want to leave?"

"Enough said. I've shared too much already. Few know this much, and I'd like to keep it that way."

"Understood."

"What about you? You're a well-endowed, handsome man. Why do you live alone? Haven't you found that perfect maiden?"

"I have one in mind. It's really a question of timing."

"Your idea?"

"No."

"Her's?"

"No."

"Who then?"

"The king."

"I see. It could only be the lovely Ariana. A good choice."

"She's a princess and I'm a blacksmith, so it's really just a dream, but a hopeful one."

"Maybe, maybe not, you have to trust in the fate of the gods."

"I have no gods, so a man's fate lies in his own hands."

"Either way, it's still fate. Trust in your instincts, and never let go of your dream. Anything is possible, what have you got to lose?"

The blacksmith returned a simple smile and picked up the necklace, leaving his company to await his repair of the damage. Scota sat briefly before following his path to the window and watched him ply his trade. He was as intriguing to her as she was to him. She admired his ethics through the glass, thinking Aiden and Ariana would be a good match. Once she saw the blacksmith returning, she reverted back to the table to wait. Scota inspected the chain and her approval was evident. She put the medallion around her neck, concealing it beneath her clothing.

"What do I owe you?"

"Conversation, I'd like to hear more of your story."

"Done, but another time, another place."

Aiden escorted Scota to her horse, boosting her to the saddle and watched her ride away. He knew she was requesting he pay the next visit. When he returned to the cottage to grab his gloves, he discovered a deep-purple amethyst lying in the middle of the table. He was surprised and yet he wasn't. There was more to her story that he had to hear.

The remainder of the week was spent pounding the sword into shape and giving it detail. Since the amethyst was a gift, he added it to the hilt for that final touch. The gem was the perfect addition and the sword a work of art. He was confident the blade would have no problem passing the king's inspection.

Finally came the morning of Gideon's sixteenth birthday. It was a beautiful day for a festive celebration, undoubtedly the biggest event to take place in the kingdom in years. The last gathering was the queen's funeral, which Aiden attended with his father some five years ago, and a joyful event was long overdue.

The blacksmith dressed in his best leather as comfortable was good. Few knew he was also a tanner, but one had to make what he couldn't afford or barter his trade to satisfy his needs. Leather had a way of enhancing a man's stature, somewhat daunting yet handsome as well.

The castle was an easy two-hour ride, passing through villages along the way. The activities were anything but subtle; mothers chasing children to keep their best clean, wagons being loaded and hitched to horses. The frenzied pace was too much for Aiden, so he rode through as quickly as possible.

As the castle came into view, red dragon flags flew from the twin turrets, three on each. Smoke rose from the many campfires of the exterior encampment, and tents of the distant travelers dotted the landscape. Aiden wasn't big on crowds, but he did enjoy people-watching, and there were more people present than he ever could have imagined.

He dismounted, tethered his horse to an unoccupied birch, and untied the wrapped blanket from the back of the saddle. As he walked leisurely toward the main gates, he couldn't help but notice the number of guards manning the walls. He strolled across the meadow, greeting friends, customers, and strangers alike. Being on king's business, Aiden was met and escorted by a guard past the crowd being filtered through the entrance to the compound. The space had become a marketplace filled with vendors by trade and merchants of various edibles. The colorful presentation was both practical and whimsical.

Entering the sanctuary, he was led down a dim candlelit corridor to the vestibule door and crossed the threshold alone. Candlesticks enhanced the light in the room, reflecting off the stained glass windows of the chamber, while highlighting the room's paintings and tapestries. The king, seated at the great table, stroked his beard and followed the blacksmith's approach with a fixed stare. Aiden laid the blanket on the table for Darian to unroll and stepped back.

"Is this the sword of swords?"

"I leave that for you to decide, sire."

"Are you without opinion?"

"Sire, my father relinquished his trade to me. I neither minimize his talent or my own."

"We shall see."

Darian untied the bundle, gazed upon the blade, and paused before securing the hilt of the sword. He stood, walking to the nearest window, to examine its balance and detail. He swung the weapon many times before holding it by the blade to analyze the impact of the light on the deep-purple stone. Aiden detected the hint of a smile as the monarch returned to the table.

"Is this the best you could do?"

"Time was inevitably the true measure of its quality, sire."

"There is no more time. Gideon's legacy will be judged this day and defined by this sword."

"Yes, sire."

"Is it worthy enough for a prince?"

"It is, if the sword pleases you."

The king silently reexamined the gift from one end to the other.

"The blade is exquisite. You've refined your skills and done your father proud. The sword has great balance, and the gem was a very nice touch. Gideon will indeed approve."

"Thank you, sire."

"What do I owe?"

"Sire, the amethyst was a gift to me, the sword a gift to you. Do with it what you wish."

"Nothing you wish that I can grant?"

"Just one, only the king can bequest."

"What would that be?"

"Presently, sire, I'm not at liberty to ask."

"So be it. Surely, we'll have dealings in the future. Go, enjoy the festival."

As Aiden departed the chamber, he knew the king had tested his character in an attempt to rattle his confidence. He had done his best work despite the king's verbal inference and then received his greatest compliment from the monarch. This was a memorable day indeed.

He stepped out of the darkened passageway and into the blinding sunlight, squinting his eyes through the change. Villagers scurried about the compound, which was too much activity for this early in the day. Aiden chose the solitude of the castle's stone wall, for now, settling on a thick patch of grass and leaning back comfortably against the fortification. His view from there was pure amusement as child and adult alike scampered about the grounds.

He didn't sit by himself very long until he was joined by Scota, her husband Theo, and Edric the eccentric, directly after they entered the market. Edric, the king's wizard, wore a cone-shaped hat and a cloak of blue, scattered with hundreds of small yellow stars. The sorcerer, in his midfifties, had long fiery-red hair and beard tied into multiple knots. His color was most unnatural, subject to dyes and reputed to change, depending on his mood, message, or whim.

Aiden met their arrival with a handshake except for the wizard who was given a verbal greeting. It was widely known that he never made physical contact.

"I thank you for leaving me the amethyst. It made a fine finish to the hilt of Gideon's sword."

"My pleasure, thanks for the repair, the conversation, and the view."

"Water does have a way of cleansing the soul, does it not?"

"It was naturally pleasing and nature at its best."

Aiden knew he would never live it down, so he just went with the moment, the two having fun at the others' expense. It was totally innocent in every way, a verbal duel, so to speak, and so far, Scota was winning the joust.

"Edric the red, is there significance in the color on such a fine day?"

"Aiden, you know there's always meaning in my message. Today, the king makes an unprecedented announcement of worthy importance."

"And?"

"A quest, that's all I'm at liberty to reveal at this time."

"Does it have anything to do with Gideon's birthday?"

"Nothing at all."

"Is it common knowledge?"

"If it was, don't you think I'd be able to tell you?"

"Maybe, maybe not, you can be a man of riddles and unspoken truth."

"True, but presently, only the four of us and the royal family have any awareness of what I speak."

"A quest of red?"

"A quest of danger."

"To where and for what?"

"Patience, you'll find out soon enough."

Their conversation was interrupted by horns, announcing the arrival of the king's entourage to the portico. All three children accompanied the king; Gideon on his left, Ariana and Camille on his right. Camille was the youngest, three years Gideon's junior, and a youthful version of her sister. Darian, wearing his crown, took a seat at his portable throne, silencing the announcement and signaling the commencement of the festivities.

The merriment began with three daring fire-breathers, spewing their flames high in the air, captivating the youngest in the crowd. A sword swallower followed. His talent, although entertaining and more dangerous, received a less stimulating response. Young girls from the village were next, decked in their colorful dresses. They danced and sang; their arms flapping with the spirit of birds as doves were released at the end of the routine. The doves flocked together in a circular motion from four different locations, spherically encompassing the compound three times, before flying away with a roaring cheer.

The wizard made his way to the façade of the royal stand as the crowd dispersed before him. Edric stood, arms at his sides, facing the prince. He slowly raised his arms till they were parallel to the ground, the cloak fanning out like the wings of a butterfly. Gradually, he rotated his arms to the forefront until his fingers touched, mirrored like the legs of a spider. Onlookers were captivated by his every move, anticipating something magical. The wizard drew his hands back behind his head, then thrust them forward, fingers extended, creating a discharge of energy, an explosive flash of light, and a cloud of smoke. The adults were awed while the children were startled.

Before the smoke could clear, the wizard reached into the cloud, pulling out his gift to the prince. His offering, still clasped in his hands, awaited Gideon's acceptance. The prince, doing his best to restrain his excitement, paced toward Edric, and accepted his first present, a pair of embellished leather gloves with fingers removed and a headband to match. Gideon's gratitude was evident, yet somewhat subdued.

Edric bowed to the prince and slowly backed away, making room for subsequent bearers. Over the next couple hours, the prince received a multitude of fine gifts from garments to glass until only the family remained. Ariana went first, giving her brother a new bow, while Camille offered the prince a quiver full of arrows. With all the focus on Gideon, Ariana still managed to flash Aiden a glance.

With bow in hand and quiver over his shoulder, the king signaled for the archery competition to begin. The targets, both moving and stationary, would challenge the highly talented field. The prince finished second out of two dozen, losing to

Tobias of the king's guard, who won the contest by splitting one of his own arrows. A very respectable finish for Gideon, and the ale flowed freely.

The king was last to present. He had his son close his eyes and extend his arms as he approached, laying the heavy sword in Gideon's hands. The prince immediately opened his eyes with the biggest of grins. He inspected the blade with great detail, especially the stone, before swinging the weapon across his body several times. Gideon was happy and his father was pleased.

Darian wasted no time selecting one of his personal guards to face the prince in a duel. Gideon wasn't new to a blade, only new to this one. The match began at a modest pace, allowing the prince time to adjust to the weight and balance of his new sword. Unlike previous blades, this was a two-handed weapon, and as he became more at ease, the contest became more serious. The guard's blade was no match for the weight of Gideon's, and the prince began to dominate, affecting his challenger's balance and finally knocking the sword out of his hands. The king was delighted. The prince had never exhibited such skill before the commoners, and his ability was more than impressive.

Gideon refilled his father's mug with ale as well as his own and prepared for the celebration to continue. Jugglers began the entertainment, tossing knives, sticks of fire, and anything else the villagers could think up. The final events of the day were designed for the children. Sack races, egg tosses, and the most popular of all was catching the greased piglet. In the end, not one child was clean despite their fussing parents.

Horns sounded once again. Aiden knew the time had finally arrived for the king's announcement and time for the blacksmith to get a much closer look. Darian stepped forward with the princess, clasping Ariana's hand in his. Silence swept over the compound in anticipation of the royal announcement. Little did they know that the message would be an unprecedented action by the realm.

"Hear ye, hear ye, this day a new declaration by the king," spoke the royal minister.

Phoenix Quest

"I thank all for your collaboration in this momentous celebration on Gideon's behalf. Let it be said, well done. There are other matters before this court, matters I've chosen to address this day. My daughter, Ariana, of childbearing age, is not yet wed. I have searched, in vain, for a sovereign suitor, worthy of her hand, only to find that none exist. Therefore, I make the following marriage proclamation. From this day forward, commencing a week hence and lasting no more than three years. Whoever shall be the first to bring me a feather of the phoenix shall prove themselves worthy of my daughter's hand and position in my court. All interested suitors must declare before accepting this quest, which shall begin from this compound in one week."

Aiden could hardly believe his ears. The impossible just became possible. He could win the hand of the princess on his own merits. It wouldn't be easy, no matter how confident he might be, and there was no way to tell how many contenders would declare, all pursuing the same end, making this quest more dangerous and challenging.

Six had already declared, prior to Aiden, including Tobias. He was an ugly sort, aggressively arrogant, vain, and rough around the edges. He was obviously displeased with the blacksmith's contention. There was a glare in his eyes and a challenge in his stance, even though the two had no history. No words were needed to express the moment, and surely, there would be confrontation somewhere down the road.

Aiden focused his attention back to the princess who, by all accounts, appeared content with her father's announcement and pleased with his declaration. Again, no words were needed to express the significance of their eye contact. They had a connection, something the blacksmith felt all along. Her approval would serve to give him strength, drive his ambition, and feed his determination.

Many people began to leave the all-day event once the royals retreated to the castle except those who would stay until the ale ran out. They would milk the festivities for all its worth. Aiden was surprised the king didn't allow the princess any parting words and hoped they might come the following week. He bid good-bye to the wizard and promised Scota a visit prior to the quest.

While Aiden walked to his horse, his thoughts wandered through the events of the day. There were more questions raised than answered. The princess was available, but where would he find a phoenix? What if he returned empty-handed or someone else found the feather that he could not? He had to remain positive as he made the quick trot home, with much to plan and prepare.

The blacksmith knew the quest had risk, even death. Unscrupulous men were capable of anything, given the right conditions. The quest wasn't just about nuptials either; it was about power and status, a measure more significant than the hand of the princess, which could put her in danger. He would have to prepare for anything, even the possibility of defending the princess after the quest.

A sword alone wouldn't be enough to assure a man's survival. Aiden already had a box of stars and his bow, but he would need more, two daggers and a breastplate more along with additional arrows. With a week to forge, there was no time to waste. The daggers would be easy; they didn't have to be intricate, just practical. The breastplate was a different story. He'd never made one before, and it had to fit his form perfectly.

After two long days and late nights, work had become his only routine; the knives were complete and the chest armor was taking shape. It had to be thin enough to be lightweight, thick enough to stop an arrow, and comfortable whether he was in battle or not. All three aspects were critical for the plate to work.

It was midafternoon on the third day, hot and humid. The blacksmith cooled off with a brief douse of his shower when he unexpectedly received another visitor. Fortunately, this time he was clad. It was Edric with a green beard while his hair remained red. He could hardly wait to hear the wizard's reasoning. He filled two mugs with ale, and they sat on a flat rock overlooking the small valley below, where the blacksmith ranged a few head of cattle. It was the first time Edric had paid Aiden a visit.

"To what do I owe this rudimentary pass?"

"I do have purpose."

"Good, let's start with your green beard."

"Earth and nature, both provide the sustenance and strength needed to survive the quest. Knowledge isn't enough, hence the red. There could be more danger and death than you know."

"I already figured that out on my own. Is there more to your purpose?"

"What if I told you, I had information that could point you in the direction of the phoenix?"

"And where would this information come from?"

"Two ways, actually. First, I have in my possession a ruby necklace said to attract the bird when the sun shines through the gem."

"Really, can I see it?"

The wizard opened his cloak and clutched a bag tied around his waist. Loosening the cord, he pulled out a long gold chain with a ruby about the size of a fist. It was cut on both sides, flat and smooth as a piece of glass about a quarter inch thick.

"How does it work?"

"Stories say the sun's rays pass through the ruby, producing a powerful beam capable of drawing the phoenix to its fiery-red glow."

"Have you ever tried to use it?"

"No, I've never had reason."

"Well, it isn't going to get any sunnier that this. Let's give it a try."

The necklace was beautiful and surprisingly heavy. Aiden held it toward the sun and was amazed by the degree of light created. The light became so bright and intense, a dried patch of grass burst into flames.

"Fire?"

"I guess, but that's not the intention. Maybe it's just a constructive consequence."

"So why do you bring this to me?"

"Because the realm would be better off with you as prince than anybody else. I want what's best for the people."

"How can you be so sure?"

"I may be eccentric, but I do possess acute perception and I'm not alone in my thoughts."

"The gem could be the edge I need."

"I can only hope. You must find the way to make it work its magic."

"Have you ever seen a phoenix or know what it looks like?"

"Never, I wish I had, that's the second reason I'm here. You must visit Scota before you leave. She's the only person I know who's ever seen the phoenix and can describe it. She can tell you where to begin your search. She knows the land and how to get there. Scota is a mysterious and powerful woman of many secrets."

"I gathered that much from our last visit."

"She feels as I do strongly, but any secrets revealed must remain so."

"I can live with that."

"More than you know. Her knowledge could save your life and shorten your quest."

Edric's visit was encouraging and gave the blacksmith a huge advantage over his rivals. With any luck at all, this adventure wouldn't be as bad as he first thought. Three years was a mammoth commitment, but now, he should be able to accomplish his goal in less time on fewer resources. The unforeseen good news left the blacksmith more motivated and confident than ever. Aiden bid the wizard good-bye with sincere gratitude and took the ruby to the cottage for safekeeping.

Another two days passed and the breastplate was done. He propped the chest protector against a stump and fired three arrows from varying distances to test its durability. None penetrated the metal, although each left a small dent in the armor. The fit was made better, knowing it would guard his life. With the metalwork complete, he shut down the forge. The only way he'd fire it up again was if he couldn't find a feather.

The blacksmith put away his tools and settled back indoors for his final preparations. He lit a fire and sat at the table. Aiden cut pieces of leather to make two sheaths, a headband, and a pair of fingerless gloves, like the ones the prince was gifted and spent the remainder of the night on assembly, knowing the morn would bring travel.

Revelations

It was early, still dark, when Aiden saddled his horse. He planned to leave at daybreak after a satisfying breakfast. It would be his first ride, along the upper road, to the coast in some time. Scota had settled there since he'd made his last trip east. The cool morning made for a good trot, and the closer he got to the coast, the more the saltwater air filled his nostrils. He could hear the waves crashing the beach, hidden by a dense fog.

The environment produced a peaceful, refreshing kind of morning as he climbed over the rise and the fog thinned. He could still see his breath, the dew on the grass, the white caps of the waves, and the soaring birds. Best of all though, he could see Scota's in the distance. The hamlet comprised more than a dozen cottages bordered by a corral, a pigsty, and chicken coops with cattle grazing on the sloping hillside. Drawing closer, he saw children feeding chickens and two males sawing and splitting logs.

Scota's village displayed a warm and welcome feeling as his unexpected arrival beckoned a gathering of greeters and waving children. Theo came forward to meet Aiden's dismount, taking his reins and handing the horse over to one of the eldest children to stable. The two shook hands as news spread through the hamlet, attracting more than fifty locals to assemble. The blacksmith had no idea the hamlet held so many residents.

These were a slightly darker-skinned people, their clothing dyed with a variety of bright, contrasting colors somewhat hidden beneath the regional attire, and jewelry of some fashion was more common than not. Theo escorted the blacksmith through the friendly reception to the largest cottage where Scota met him at the door.

He was immediately astonished by the decorum upon entering her abode. Numerous small statues were scattered about the room. The carved stone images exposed head and neck adornments, mostly busts dressed in stature, while others bore the likenesses of birds and dogs. He wondered if the statues were religious symbols or representations of everyday life; either way, they were most impressive.

The wooden floor was partially concealed by a large ornamental rug with three pyramids at its center framed by squares containing a variety of unusual images. The pyramids had a smooth white surface that gleamed in the sun, and the structures were totally encompassed by sand. Aiden took a seat on a brilliant-red pillow that lay nearby.

"So what do you think?"

"I've never seen anything like it. The presentation is very unusual."

"We're surrounded by my legacy, both past and present."

"Somehow, I feel that's the reason I'm here."

"Yes, it is, and I'm so glad you made time to call. Right now you must be overwhelmed with all that's taken place and time is fleeting."

"Edric made it quite clear, I see you, when he last visited."

"I knew he would. Everything you see around you is part of my story, a story I'm going to finish telling. A lot has changed since you repaired my necklace, and now it's become essential you hear it all."

The two faced each other from opposite sides of a short-legged table. They were served tea in small silver cups with exterior etchings. Both took sips, relaxed, and got comfortable.

"In my homeland, these statues around you exist much larger, in number and size, dwarfing a man. The two busts are those of my parents."

"They look significant."

"My real name is Meritaten. I'm a princess, the eldest of six daughters of Pharaoh Amenhotep IV and Queen Nefertiti. They rule Lower Egypt from the Nile River, which is the longest in the known world. My husband is Prince Gaytheios."

"I knew this would be a great story. Why would you leave Egypt? It sounds like you had a pretty good life."

"We held a rank of privilege, but escaped two years ago, fearing plagues would consume and collapse the country. To save our children, we disappeared under the cover of night without saying a word to my parents. We feared if they found out our plan, they would do everything in their power to prevent us from leaving."

"What kind of plagues?"

"Most likely disease, locusts, and famine. My father also wanted to change the religious practices that would impact most existing temples, priests, and which gods were worshiped. We weren't sure how his plan would be received, especially by the priests."

"Sounds like chaos."

"Indeed. We choose to hide our identity. It was easier to blend in since our positions meant nothing here. If we remained anonymous, we wouldn't have strangers knocking on our door, if you know what I mean."

"Well, you don't exactly blend in."

"True, some things are hard to relinquish. Our culture has passed down through generations. We've made changes, subtle ones, but that doesn't alter who we are. We say little, keep to ourselves, and leave the rest to imagination."

"You've sailed the inland sea and settled on the island instead of somewhere along the coast. Why here?"

"The island provides safety the mainland does not. You can only get here by boat."

"Was this your destination?"

"No, some settled on the Iberian Peninsula, but we wanted to create more distance and explore a new world beyond the sea, which brought us here. It was a predestined voyage blessed by the gods."

Aiden sensed a lot of emotion as she related her tale, and while their cups were refilled, they both enjoyed the moments of silence.

"Edric tells me you've seen the phoenix."

"Not exactly, I've seen sculptures, paintings, and glyphs, renditions that span the centuries. The arrival of the phoenix is documented by priests in the royal record at the Temple of Heliopolis."

"What do they have written in the record?"

"The phoenix has a life cycle of five hundred years. The bird returns its ashes to the Sun City, inside the temple at Heliopolis, in Egypt, after its rebirth. That's your ultimate destination."

"Rebirth?"

"The phoenix is a fire spirit. It constructs a nest of oak branches, sprinkled heavily with cinnamon, myrrh, and spikenard. Upon its demise, the bird exhales its last breath of fire on the fragrances igniting the nest with an intense flame. From the ashes, an egg is hatched, renewing life again for the next five hundred years. The remaining ashes are then carried to the temple."

"You've said five hundred years twice, I'm almost afraid to ask where I fall in the timetable."

"Fortunately for you, it's not an exact science. The day has been known to fluctuate, one way or the other, and best of all, the rebirth should take place sometime in two years."

"That's remarkable. I could be in Egypt for two years. Did the king know that?"

"He did after I told him, hence the three-year quest time frame."

"So what does a phoenix look like?"

"It's about the size of an eagle, maybe a little larger, with feathers of gold, scarlet, purple, blue, and green, somewhat like a pheasant and a rainbow. It has long legs and talons, but unlike other birds, it has small ears on top of its head. A phoenix doesn't eat fruits or vegetation, it survives on frankincense and other fragrant resins. Stories say its cry is like a beautiful song, and others put forth the idea the phoenix can change into human form."

"Is it aggressive?"

"I would imagine it could be threatening if agitated. It does breathe fire and that should heed caution. Nobody wants to be a pile of ashes."

"So where does it resurrect itself?"

"Stories suggest it builds the nest in the oak trees at the water of life, but nobody really knows for sure."

"Water of life?"

"Waters of healing and eternal life. Desperate men have searched for it, but only the phoenix knows its location and protects against its revelation."

"This quest actually seemed easier before I received all this new information. 'Bring me a feather of the phoenix' sounds much simpler than it really is. Anything else I should know about this mysterious and colorful creature?"

"The bird is intelligent and not likely to give up its plumage willingly. You might be able to barter, but the only thing I can think of is frankincense."

"I can only imagine how lost I'd be without your help and how disoriented my rivals will be in its lacking."

Scota assured the blacksmith that no others possessed the details he had, not even Edric, and the king only knew the phoenix existed. Their mugs were refilled, and they began to walk about the room, the princess of Egypt explaining the sculptures, the meanings beyond the symbols, and the significance of the three pyramids before returning to the pillows where Theo joined them, map in hand.

"The prince sailed us through the dangers of the inland sea, the unpredictable oceans' storms, and along the rugged island coastline, avoiding the certain death of the rocks. The twelve-day voyage wasn't easy, but with the blessing of the gods, we made it."

The prince unfolded the map and spread it out across the table between them. The map, tracing their voyage from Egypt, was the most detailed chart Aiden had ever seen. It showed the immense size of the inland sea, the Pillars of Hercules, and the Celt Island's position in relationship to the mainland. The blacksmith's eyes were opened to the vastness of the unknown world he was about to travel, having never been off the island.

Flat bread and sardines were served, putting the travels on hold for a time. Aiden explained the projects of his week, laying his twin daggers on the table for their inspection and producing the crown jewel the wizard had given him. All three went outside to view its red brilliance as he shared its proposed functional purpose of attracting the phoenix.

"I've never heard that theory before," Scota admitted, "but the design looks familiar. I think it's Mycenaean."

"Maybe I've found my gift to barter for a feather."

"You won't know until you try."

They returned back inside so Theo could recount their journey and set the blacksmith's course.

"Crossing the channel to the mainland can have dangerously swift currents, depending on the weather and you don't want to cross in the dark. There are settlements along the coast you probably want to avoid. I don't know anything about the people or even if it's safe. Just keep sailing until you pass through the Pillars of Hercules and enter the inland sea. As you can see, it's full of islands, and most have safe harbors for travelers. Some have cultures like Egypt, thousands of years old, and their civilizations far more advanced than we are here. All the islands in the region trade with each other, so you might be able to gain information along the way. You can get water and supplies here. The Balearic Islands are known for their pottery, agriculture, and slings. The nice things about slings, you never run out of stones, and once you learn how to use one, they're very accurate at a distance. This time of year, some residents are known to farm in the nude."

"I bet that's a sight. I see there are at least five islands. Does it matter which one I port?"

"The biggest port is on the largest island, other than that, no difference but size."

"Where next?"

"You'll pass by the island of Thrinacia at the base of the boot. It's the largest island in the sea, where Helios's sacred cattle graze. It's also home for the world's largest active volcano, Mount Aetna, which has a history of eruptions."

"I'm not familiar with volcanoes."

"Think of it in blacksmith terms. Your forge heats the metal till it's red-hot and pliable. With volcanoes, lava gets so hot it becomes a molten liquid, spewing out the top and flowing down the sides. The eruption is devastating, but Aetna isn't the only volcano in the region."

"Any recent eruptions?"

"Not on Thrinacia, but there was an eruption on Thera, an island in the Mycenaean Empire a hundred years ago. It destroyed the civilization in Malta, your next stop. Malta has the regions oldest-known temple, a few thousand years old, and monoliths sticking out of the ground that could even be older. The island was known for its fertility cult, a strange religion, since their culture and society disappeared fifty years before Thera erupted. Nobody knows how or why, they're just gone. Maybe their fertility goddess let them down. The island does have new villages that were settled since that time."

"So far, all these islands have something strange or unusual about them."

"Diverse cultures have different beliefs, and we haven't reached Egypt yet. Crete used to be the Minoan Empire until it was conquered by the Mycenaeans around the same time Thera erupted. The eruption collapsed many buildings and most of the temples, although some have been rebuilt. The island's seaports handle the bulk of merchant shipping in the region. They export ceramics, fabric, dyes, and precious gems mostly to Egypt. We trade papyrus, wheat, and cattle in return. They worship the bull, its image is found everywhere in their architecture and temples. You must see the bull dance ceremony while you're there.

"The Mycenaean Empire lies to the north with Thera being one of more than a hundred islands. On the mainland, they have a fortress in Athens. Their armies are one of the most disciplined in the world and trained from an early age. They have the largest fleet of merchant ships if you're in need of transport. The Mycenaean's have gods and creatures for everything, like Egypt, but it seems to be more about nature, strength, and myth than it has about religion. Most of them possess unearthly abilities. The gods reside at Mount Olympus while the creatures could be anywhere. I don't know how real it all is."

"Describe what you mean by unearthly abilities? It sounds threatening."

"Sea monsters, sirens, giants, and creatures with wings, which should never be allowed to fly. Things I've heard about, but never seen myself."

"I only hope I can claim the same."

"Finally, Egypt and the Blue Nile. The river is critical to Egypt's place in the world and the longest river known to man. You'll have to sail up the delta to the city of Mennefer. The city's been the center of Egyptian rule for generations of pharaohs, filled with palaces and temples, unmatched by any culture. More people live there than you've ever seen and the sphinx and pyramids are only a short distance away at Giza.

"Heliopolis, the Sun City, was also built on the Nile delta, just north of Mennefer. It too used to be the center of Egyptian rule. With the eighteenth dynasty of pharaohs, the center has shifted farther down the Nile. Amenhotep IV built his first temple in Amarna and is working on a second in Thebes farther upriver near the Valley of the Kings."

"How many temples does one man need?"

"In Egypt's case, as many as they want. Palaces and temples of historical importance exist up and down the river, all built at the whim of each ruling pharaoh, but none as important as the temple at Heliopolis. Its importance as a religious center hasn't changed over the generations. The temple attracts hundreds of thousands of Egyptians and other visitors, mainly in the winter months, due to the fact it stores a majority of the country's grain supply. So now you know all about us, where you're going, and how to get there."

James Malcolm

"I'd like to hear more about Egypt since that's my destination. The more I know, the better I'm prepared."

"If you wish. Egypt is powerfully rich with thousands of years of history and culture, affluent in the sciences, medicine, weaponry, and builders of the most spectacular architecture in the world. Craftsmen work in glass, marble, and every metal known to man.

"Egyptians, also have many gods, but have a tendency to worship one at a time. Atum is worshiped as the first deity god, self-created. He is the god of the evening sun, father of the pharaohs, and the creator who lifts the king's soul from his tomb to the heavens and afterlife. The Sun Temple in Heliopolis was built to worship him.

"Ra is also a first deity god and worshiped as a creator. He is the sun god and represents light, warmth, and growth. He too has a temple in Heliopolis.

"You've seen the rug with the pyramids at Giza. Tombs of the pharaohs that built them rest inside, safe from looters. Priests mummified their pharaohs and buried them with all their personal possessions for their use in the afterlife. Smaller pyramids exist up and down the river, and new burials are now taking place in the Valley of the Kings.

"I could keep going all day. I've given you the basic information you need for the quest, the rest you'll learn along the way. If you're done with that tea, it's time for a man's drink."

"My success on this quest will be measured by the information you've unselfishly given me, and I can't thank you enough. I'm as prepared as I can be, except for one thing. I can't begin a voyage without a boat."

"We have boats, hidden away. One is yours for the journey, but you can't sail by yourself. We'll supply a crew to get you as far as the Balearic Islands. Use the merchant ships to get to Egypt from there. You'll also need to find your own way home."

"When do we sail?"

"As soon as the king commences the quest. Every man that declares has to find a way off the island. You're better off having them behind you than at your front."

"Agreed. How I can ever thank you?"

"Well," Scota paused. "I do have one request."

"Anything."

"I want you to take my necklace and give it to my father. I want him to know we're alive and well. The necklace will also serve as proof that we sent you to Egypt with our blessings. My father and his priests should provide you access that others might deny and grant you accommodations in the many palaces during your quest."

"Done, but your request does more to benefit me, so I'm not really doing you the favor."

"As my personal messenger, you are."

Aiden took the necklace and tucked it in his sack. He felt privileged to take Meritaten's message to her father and couldn't wait to begin his travels, but for now, he would enjoy the drink and the company of his friends. The day progressed and soon it became time to leave; the three agreed to meet at the castle early the next morning. Aiden retrieved his freshly groomed horse and headed back home.

His excitement made sleep difficult, so he packed and prepared for an early morning departure, then lay in front of the fireplace, enjoying the dancing flames, and retraced the unbelievable sequence of events that had gotten him to this point.

The day was finally here and Aiden was feeling anxious. He took one last look at his cottage and rode off at a gallop. It would be sometime before he saw home again, but with any luck, home would become the castle and that was an intoxicating thought.

The turnout at the castle was almost as big as Gideon's birthday. Everyone was curious about the start of the quest and who had declared. They were waiting for the king, who was still in the castle, and the crowd continued to grow. Aiden was sizing up his competition. Some of his rivals were obvious while others were not. Tobias was talking with his squire and hadn't noticed the blacksmith's arrival.

The wizard was the first to make an appearance, exiting from the castle, and eventually spotted Aiden leaning against the stone wall. Edric's beard was now blue while his hair remained red. As he made his approach, Scota and Theo made their first appearance, entering the front gate.

"Edric the blue, how do you do."

"Now you're a poet?"

"We both know there's no future in that."

"Blue future is more exact, nobody gets off the island without crossing the troubled waters."

"Do you think everyone here will find a boat?"

"Look at some of these fools. They don't know they need a boat. Some don't realize they need to leave the island on this quest."

The wizard knew more about who had declared than he did, taking the liberty to point out a few to prove his point. Some were too young, others too old, one short and fat, while two were tall and skinny. Not at all what one would expect to find on a quest, but then, there were also many serious contenders like Tobias. The quest was open to everyone.

"You've come from the castle. Do you know how long before the king comes forward?"

"Soon."

The prince and princess of Egypt joined them at the wall. The wizard was updated on the visit from the day before, events surpassing even Edric's expectation. Then horns sounded, proclaiming the beginning of the beginning as the king would put an end to Aiden's wait.

"Hear ye, hear ye. King Darian's proclamation. All declared, please step forward."

The blacksmith proceeded toward the stage, with encouragement from his friends. It was time to find out who would content for the hand of the princess and those who would oppose his pursuits. Aiden studied those moving forward as they formed a line facing the stand, his count interrupted by Darian's entrance with Ariana in hand.

"Greetings on this day of great magnitude. Before me stand those who feel themselves worthy of this monumental challenge, but only one shall triumph. The fittest of the fit will be tested and the bravest of the brave will face consequence. I hereby demand reputation and honor be forthwith, on behalf of my daughter, to truly be worthy. May wisdom and judgment be with each of you and safeguard your lives. The princess shall speak with each of you, in turn, before I proclaim this quest go forward."

Anticipation swept over Aiden. He'd never spoken a word to the princess before. He wasn't sure what to expect, from her or himself. The blacksmith watched her work her way closer as she moved down the line. She smiled and greeted each one in turn without touching. He took a moment to finalize his count. Thirty-eight stood to receive her, counting him, a larger number than he had foreseen, and now he was next.

For the first time in his life, he felt nervous. The princess stepped to face him, toe to toe and eye to eye. The emotion he experienced was indescribable, and he tried maintaining reasonable composure. She was more beautiful than he'd seen at a distance, with blue eyes, smooth skin, and soft voice.

"Aiden."

"Princess."

"I must tell you, I've looked forward to this day."

"This day is all about you, princess. It's why we're all here."

"I would be pleased if you addressed me by Ariana, I've long wanted to converse, but imagined it in a much different way."

"I am truly honored, really."

"And I am grateful you declared, Aiden. You can do this, and my heart goes with you."

"If I can be so bold, it's for your heart I declare."

"That's why everyone declared, you're no different."

"I'm very different."

"I know you are. Be safe. You've already won my heart, now win this quest."

"Your hope is my dream, princess."

The princess gave the blacksmith an enduring smile before moving on down the line. He wanted to touch her and felt she had the same sensation, but neither could act on the impulse. He never expected the princess to reveal herself so freely, but couldn't have been more convinced by her sentiment that he didn't have to worry about winning her heart; he had to win the quest. He watched her go from one challenger to the next, still absorbing the gravity of their conversation and wondering what she was saying to the others in a more contrite discussion. Aiden could feel his heart pounding out of his chest, still stunned by the openness of their meeting.

Aiden couldn't help but follow her progress until she'd reached the last in line. Ariana returned to her father's side, taking his hand once more. Then the king made the same gesture, following her steps down the row of declarers. Aiden was grateful the king hadn't chosen to walk with his daughter, or she wouldn't have been so forthright with her feelings. Maybe there was purpose to which he was unaware or maybe he let her have her own parting words, not influenced by his presence.

"Aiden."

"Sire."

"Be the man I know you are."

The king shook his hand and moved on. Aiden wondered if his message was a general comment or was there more in his words. He'd like to think the latter for his sake. Now all the blacksmith could focus on was the princess. He couldn't take his eyes off her. She returned his attention, but less obvious, for all the right reasons and then the king rejoined her.

"May each man be sound in body and remain honorable in the spirit of this quest. Your actions will reflect on the kingdom. Be upright ambassadors and return home safely. Let the quest begin."

Each contender bowed, then the scene became one of frenzied disarray. Half took off running like it was a race instead of a journey halfway around the world. Did they know where they were going and how they were going to get there, or was Edric right, these were the ones with no idea or plan? Aiden, still smitten, held his ground like he was under a spell, unaware that Tobias approached.

"Stay out of my way, blacksmith."

Aiden wasn't surprised by the outburst. In fact, he'd rather have it said now than later. He didn't care to see Tobias again, either, until this whole thing was over. He gave the princess one more long look and left her presence to join Scota, Theo, and Edric.

"Well, it appears that went off without a hitch," Scota scoffed.

"The hitch takes place when I get back."

"Are you ready to go?"

"I'm as ready as I'll ever be."

"There is one more thing I'm required to give you, Aiden, before you leave."

"What more could I possibly need, wizard?"

"Something to make your days shorter and nights longer."

"What have you conjured up?"

"Nothing, it's not even my idea."

"What then?"

"I couldn't help notice how long the princess was occupied and overwhelmed by your charm."

"Me either. You should have been there."

"You earned your moment, undisturbed by the likes of me."

"So what is it you have with the power to impact my days and nights?"

"A hanky belonging to a fair young maiden."

"And how did you obtain this hanky?"

"It was given, from her hand to mine, with instructions, not to bestow until now."

Aiden was again stunned by the conduct of the princess. Her behavior was bold in a good way. He wasn't threatened by her outspoken nature, but rather admired it. She was unafraid to show her feelings and confident enough to make the first move. Something more difficult for the blacksmith to do, considering his position.

The blacksmith's day couldn't have been more unpredictable or gratifying. The princess had validated him in every way. He had the ruby, a map, her hanky, and her heart. Aiden was given every advantage to succeed in this quest. His friends and the princess had seen to that. They would all travel with him in their own way.

The wizard had parting words, and the blacksmith was ready to go. He rode with the Egyptians to their hamlet with the princess being the topic of every conversation until there was nothing left to say. The moments of silence were precious and few, given Aiden's ardently animated state of mind. His passion for life had become passionate, and Scota found him adorable. He had a soft side to his rugged exterior and vulnerability in his heart. Theo, on the other hand, was concerned about focus, keeping it centered and pointed in the right direction. The blacksmith didn't need excessive distractions on his perilous journey.

Arriving at the village, Aiden dismounted and wrapped his arms around the neck of his horse, whispering in his ear. It would be the last they would see each other for some time. His steed was in good hands as were the cattle and horses left at his cottage. Scota gave Aiden a parting hug, and he proceeded to the shoreline with Theo and his crew of seven, loaded down with gear.

The party walked up the beach a couple hundred yards to the largest pile of driftwood stacked against the bank. Aiden watched the Egyptians unstack the logs until a dugout cave was revealed. It was hard to tell how deep it went, but the width was at least a dozen feet. The roof was framed with small timbers, piled high with branches. They grabbed the end of a rope and began to pull. The blacksmith joined in the tug as the bow of a vessel slowly became visible.

At first, the slide was only inches at a time until they could lift the boat, enough to begin rolling small logs underneath. The more logs, the faster it slid, exposing a craft some thirty feet long, complete with a mast and oars, resting on the seats and rolled sail alongside.

In no time at all, the logs were doing all the work, and waves began washing against the bow. The boat was eased into water and anchored to a rock. Together, they raised the mast and attached the striped sail of blue and golden yellow. Once all the supplies for the voyage were loaded aboard the vessel, it was time to set sail.

Jib, Scota's cousin, would lead the voyage to the inland sea. He was tall with a shaved head and a braided, shoulder-length tuft of hair. Scars marked the right forearm and left thigh of this battle-tested warrior. Jib was the type of soldier one would want by his side in a fight. Hondo also had a scar on his right cheek, and the small finger on his right hand was missing. It was hard to tell whether the other five had seen any conflict. Either way, Aiden felt like he was in good company.

Lorelei's Enchantment

The Egyptians said last good-byes to their loved ones, and the eight travelers shoved off. The quest was finally underway as a light wind caught the sail, and the detail of island gradually became an outline. The seasoned sailors had made this journey before, giving Aiden peace of mind and time to learn some seafaring skills.

Their eastern heading brought more turbulent water, and it was only a matter of time before the blacksmith was heaving over the bow. As he raised his head, he saw something floating between the rolling waves. At first it was hard to ascertain the debris, and as they drew closer, it wasn't wreckage at all. A small overturned boat drifted helplessly with two bodies floating nearby. They dropped the sail momentarily, manning the oars to get a closer look. Aiden, still leaning over the side, rolled the first corpse over and then moved on to the second.

"They are both young declarers of the quest."

"This is what happens when you're ill prepared. That boat is too small for a crossing like this, and it's likely neither young man had any nautical skills," Jib responded.

"Too bad, drowning out here, their families will never know until someone returns to give them the heartbreaking news."

"A sad result of poor strategy."

The sails were raised again, and they didn't travel far before passing by a third victim of the ill-fated crossing. The blacksmith wondered why three competitors would put to sea in such an unworthy craft. Was there a shortage of boats or just a lack in judgment?

Winds picked up as their vessel reached the halfway point of the channel, and the rougher water caused one Egyptian to puke over the side. Aiden was glad he wasn't the only one to humiliate himself on this voyage. Obviously, neither one had sea legs nor the sense to skip breakfast, but the blacksmith was determined not to repeat the experience. Suddenly, without warning, there was a huge splash, forty feet off the port side.

"What was that?" Aidan questioned, wondering if tales of sea monsters would sink their craft.

"Someone's firing at us," Jib answered as he made out the sail of a larger vessel behind them.

"Firing with what? They're so far away."

"It's a catapult, capable of firing anything they want."

"The damn thing's pretty accurate."

"That was only a mark volley, the next one will be closer."

No sooner had Jib spoken, there was a second splash; this time, it was ten feet closer. Staying on the water wasn't going to be a good option. They had to make shore, if possible, with no means to defend themselves from a ship that had them outclassed. Aiden could hear the third volley sing as it flew through the air. A flaming ball of fire with a trail of smoke landed ten feet off the bow, close enough to get him wet.

Hondo turned the rudder sharply, changing the line of fire, and steered with the current to maintain their speed. They were being outpaced by the larger enemy ship, and the coastline was a mere outline. If they couldn't make land, the battle would be fought at sea, blade to blade, unless a volley sank them first.

"Might be pirates and they have no loyalty to anyone, including each other," Jib theorized, "They can be a nasty bunch."

Another volley was lobbed, barely clearing the mast, and again, they were doused with water. Gusts of wind caught their sail, sending the boat knifing through the waves. The enemy ship was heavier and drew more water; with luck, maybe the weight would be enough to give the smaller boat a speed advantage. The coast was still a distant objective, although it grew nearer and more detailed by the minute.

A second flaming fireball was launched with deadly accuracy, strafing the portside, leaving the boat and sail on fire. Both were quickly extinguished with buckets of seawater in a frantic response, and Hondo changed their course once again. The damage to the portside wasn't as bad as it first appeared, but the imperfections of the sail would slow them down; to what degree was still unmeasured.

Just as suddenly as the wind gusted, the air went still, dead still. The sails became useless, and the boat's momentum began to slow. The crew scrambled to break out their eight oars and began rowing at a feverish pace. The enemy ship was close enough to see it had no oars in the water, and the distance between the two vessels began to widen. The calm was helping them survive the vicious attack; the longer it lasted made reaching the coast a distinct reality.

Jib asked Hondo for his shirt to repair the sail, which he gladly relinquished to the cause. Two additional small holes were cut in the sail, and the shirt was tied into the burned-out corner. It wasn't perfect, but the simple mend would catch more air. Aiden was impressed by the clever and creative craftsmanship. After picking up at least ten boat lengths on the marauders, the wind kicked up again and the crew stowed the oars.

The shirt was working, and the coast was within two miles. If they had to fight, they stood a better chance with their feet on solid ground. Another volley was fired to mark the fleeing vessel, this time it wasn't even close, so Hondo kept them on their current course. An additional mark was fired, cutting the distance of the first miss in half, and Hondo made another adjustment.

The pirates began to close the gap again with the mainland a mere mile away. They lobbed another mark, and it sang as it plunged from overhead. It struck the boat dead center, missing the mast, but leaving a hole in the hull. Jib quickly grabbed a bucket and stomped it in the gap, slowing the deluge to a manageable trickle. The next attempt would likely be fire, a hit they couldn't afford to sustain. It would devastate their vessel and surely cost lives. The once-distant shores now had detail, and the crew would make land in time if they didn't suffer another strike.

"What's our strategy when we land? Do we make a stand?" Aiden asked Jib.

"I can't answer that until I see their number."

"How close will they need to get before we know that?"

"I'll have a better idea when we know the length of their ship."

"And if we're outnumbered?"

"Then we beach the boat and survive to fight another day."

"They will destroy the boat."

"They'll burn it while we'll make our escape on foot."

"It looks like I'll have company on this quest after all, and I thought I'd be on my own."

"Only as long as it takes to find adequate transport home."

"Right, but until then, we're linked."

"Hondo, change our heading so we can judge their length and draw."

The maneuver revealed a lengthy vessel more than twice their size, capable of carrying three times their crew. It became clear that escape was their only option and standing their ground would only result in certain death. They were close enough to the shore now for the waves to have whitecaps and the waters to become shallow. The crew would have to bail out before beaching the boat, so they gathered their gear and supplies together in readiness.

They were jumping in the water as soon as the craft struck the rocky bottom. Waist-deep in the cold water, they struggled toward the beach. One last fireball made another direct hit, snapping the mast and engulfing the boat in a blazing inferno. Their deadly adversaries were still a couple hundred yards offshore when they reached the beach. Climbing over rocks and driftwood, they made their own trail through the dense underbrush in a desperate sprint to the tree line.

Reaching the woods, they took a defensive stand behind trees, armed with bows, and waited for the marauders to reach the thicket. Their deadly aim would reverse the fate delivered at the hands of the pirates. They waited patiently to launch the barrage of arrows in their own surprise attack. The sun was high and sweat began to run down Aiden's brow. He'd never fired an arrow at anyone before, but survival left him no other choice. It would be a worthy test of skill, one of many the blacksmith could face going forward.

The bobbing heads of the enemy were visible as they reached the rocks and logs scattered along the beach. Each had long scraggly hair, some with crude helmets. They climbed up the bank, dressed in animal skins and armed only with swords having wide but shorter blades. Jib was right about their number. There were at least thirty worthy opponents; they had to be kept at a distance. Aiden's concentration was broken by Jib's tap on the shoulder.

"Three arrows and we leave to find higher ground."

The blacksmith answered with a nod, then returned to his aim. Half the pirates had reached the high ground of the thicket, making their own paths as they charged toward the trees.

"Now!"

Arrows flew with fatal precision, most striking the chest and dropping the targets where they stood. The second and third arrows were less accurate, striking limbs, shoulders, and some near misses as the enemy sought a defensive position. Seven were down, and they were still outnumbered, although their odds had improved. Now they faced an impaired, pissed enemy, which was more dangerous.

Jib, Aiden, and two members of the crew ran deeper into the forest to find another offensive position to launch more damage while the remainder stayed with Hondo to cover their escape. With two more arrows each, they waited for a second assault, which was delayed while the pirates tried to regroup.

A hundred yards into the woods, two walls of rock covered with moss emerged, large in scale and in line with the beach. They scrambled up a rocky crevice between the walls, holding the higher ground and preparing for the others to join them. They gathered what few large rocks they could carry to toss from the ledge on the chance their foes got close enough to leave arrows ineffective.

Hondo tried to ascertain the movement on the beach. Strategy was being played out as he heard them argue among themselves, and some appeared uncertain with the results. They broke into three smaller groups; one stayed firm while the others went up or down the shore.

"Concentrate on the center," Hondo declared.

The attack began from the flanks at a safe distance with a charge straight for the tree line. The middle assault waited until their comrades had reached the forest before they made their move. Their charge started with a lengthy crawl before rising to their feet.

"Only two and make them count," Hondo whispered.

Arrows raced toward the core targets as the flanks were closing in from both sides. Three more deadly strikes and the Egyptians were on the run with pirates from the flanks tracing their steps. The separation was small, and Hondo counted on Jib to give them cover once they reached the undisclosed rendezvous. It was a race of the fittest, with the Egyptians widening the gap ever so slightly. The nearest pursuers let two axes fly, one striking Jib's trailing comrade in the back and the other buried in a tree. A casualty of war that couldn't be helped, the Egyptians had to leave him behind.

Reaching the rock walls, Jib whistled his position, and Hondo directed the others to start the ascent while he covered their climb, sword in hand. When the marauders reached the small clearing, arrows flew again, but this time, several small shields blocked most of the projectiles. Hondo engaged multiple challengers in close combat as the barrage continued from above.

"We can't leave him down there by himself," Aiden said, pulling out his twin daggers.

"I'm with you," Jib declared.

Both jumped off the short cliff, crashing into the horde below, with arrows still airborne. Aiden's daggers served him well in such close quarters. A fierce battle ensued with Hondo and Jib suffering minor wounds, and seven more of the enemy went down. Their adversaries began a retreat to regroup, giving Aiden the chance to try out his stars. He drew three from his pouch and let them fly, striking the fleeing horde's extremities before reaching down to grab two short-bladed trophy swords.

The trio scrambled back up the crevice and reunited. Jib's right shoulder dripped blood from a deep gash. He ripped the tail of his shirt and, with the blacksmith's help, tied off the wound. Hondo's less serious laceration, from a glancing blow, was also dressed.

"We can't stay here. We need to go," Jib advised.

"We've still got the high ground," Aiden replied.

"I'm sure they're not stupid. They won't try another frontal assault when they can swing around behind us and reduce their losses."

"You're right, a sheer drop at our backs would make us most vulnerable."

They went north first before going deeper into woods, hoping to throw off their pursuers. The rapid pace served to put distance between the two rivals, and they never crossed paths again. They made their way across a large meadow, setting up camp on the far side and posting sentries. They could still see the faint trail of smoke from their burning boat, hovering over the forest.

Jib washed his wound and cauterized it with a hot blade. The Egyptian's toughness seemed unfazed as Aiden stitched the gash closed. It had been one hell of a day. They fought with dignity and purpose, overcoming great odds, but they lost one of their own.

Breaking camp, they continued on their eastern heading for half the day before arriving at a wide river flowing west. Walking upstream a short distance, they took a break where large rocks lined the riverbed. They bathed fully clothed, washing the conflict blood from their skin and cleaning up their weapons before starting out again.

The pace was relaxed, but guarded. They were crossing unexplored territory of unknown inhabitants and had to avoid any repeat like the day before. The party continued following the crooked path of the river until finding a suitable site to settle for the night. It was still daylight when Aiden and Jib went on a two-man hunting party returning with a doe the blacksmith dropped with a single arrow and roasted the deer on a makeshift spit.

Morning was cloudy with a light refreshing rain. Both hindquarters of venison were tied together, and the travelers resumed their trek inland. Not long into the journey, smoke was spotted, rising just around the next bend. Cautiously, they eased forward under the cover of the canopy to get a better look.

The village was a crude assortment of tents with inhabitants in makeshift attire. They appeared to be a simple people, vagabonds by the looks of it, and no weapons were visible. Their mobile community looked safe enough for the party to penetrate in a noninvasive manner. The venison would serve them well in this endeavor and give them the opportunity to gather what information they could about the territory.

Slowly with no sudden movements, they entered the village, constantly nodding their heads in a friendly manner. Startled at first, the natives pulled back and gathered in a cluster. Hondo took the meat and cut the rope, offering a hindquarter in good faith. He stepped forward, laid the venison down, and changed their cool reception.

"We mean no harm."

"You're a strange-looking bunch," an elder was quick to point out.

"Likewise."

Hondo shook his hand and the rest followed in turn. The huddle of villagers moved forward, more curious than frightened of the strangely dressed foreigners.

"You must have traveled far, very far by the looks of your threads and weapons."

"Yes and no, some of us have traveled farther than others," Aiden answered.

"How distant?"

The blacksmith gave him the short version of their story, and as would be expected, they knew nothing of the island or the inland sea. He shared their encounter with the pirates and found the village had been raided in the past, mostly for their women. The description was similar, but two summers had passed since the last attack. They were river vagabonds who never ventured to the coast, so they hadn't seen their abductors' boats.

"We are grateful for the meat."

"We had more than we needed."

The elder's name was Bird, explaining the nickname was his mother's choice because he was both needy and agitated as a child, so he kept it. The afternoon was spent mingling and satisfying the children's inquisitive nature before sitting down with the elders and a serious conversation initiated by Jib.

"How well do you know the area?"

"Very well, I've traveled this region all my life."

"As you know, this isn't the water we intended to travel, but since our voyage to the inland sea was cut short, the river seemed like the best choice at the time. How far have you ventured upstream?"

"All the way to the great rock."

"And how far is that?"

"About five days' travel at a moderate pace."

"Do you know what lies beyond the great rock?"

"Just more river."

"Any more settlements along the way?"

"No, but there is another village that moves from place to place, like we do, because of the raids."

"How do you defend yourselves from these raids?" Aiden asked.

"We have a couple knives, but without the proper weapons, it's better to let them take what they want and move on."

Aiden went to his pack and loosened the rope that tied the two enemy swords and returned to the campfire.

"Maybe these will help."

"We don't have anyone experienced enough to use a sword."

"We can help with that. You can't let the raiders take your women. If you don't make a stand, they'll keep coming back, time and time again. Think of your daughters."

"Nobody wants to die."

"Keep them at a distance. You're surrounded by trees, make all the spears that you can. Dig pits around the village and cover them over. Do what you have to do to protect yourselves, and you won't have to keep moving all the time. Do it for your loved ones."

"It won't be easy, we've been passive so long."

"We can stay a day or two and give them some training, motivation, and confidence."

"It will take all three to change our mind-set, but any tools you give us would be valued."

"Anything more you can tell us about the river?" Jib redirected the conversation.

"Indeed, there is a siren named Lorelei. She lives in the caves along the great rock wall at the bend of the river. I've only seen the rock from a distance, and even the bravest of men avoid getting anywhere near. Lorelei's lover abandoned her, and ever since, she has enchanted and bewitched men's souls with her irresistible song."

"Is there anyway to prevent her seduction?"

"Plugging your ears so you can't hear her sing, but her song travels a vast distance. We've had men disappear and never be seen again."

"How about going around the rock to avoid her enchantment?"

"The south side of the river is the territory of a hostile tribe, so we never cross. The north side would take you days out of your way with the river winding south. If your destination requires you follow the river, then do so with caution, plug your ears, and move at a hurried pace."

The rest of the night was spent answering their questions about the island and the inland sea as they had a meal of venison, mushrooms, and berries. The clouds waned, revealing a full moon that lit up the sky and highlighted everything that surrounded them.

The next day was spent teaching villagers the proper use of a sword, and they were eager to learn. The short blades required less effort, due to their weight and balance, but they still felt uneasy and awkward, having never brandished a sword before. Motivation required heart and discipline, something hard to demonstrate in such a short time to a people of simple culture, but their standing did improve. Their progress would be measured by how they applied the skill after the teachers were gone.

That evening, several villagers provided the entertainment, showing what they'd learned. The swordfights were fun and did lift spirits, but until they took the craft more seriously, they would never reap the benefit. More stories about the inland sea nations were shared around the campfire, and Jib told the villagers they would depart the next day.

Aiden kept thinking about the siren and how best to plug his ears. There had to be a simple way to avoid her spell, so simple that he spent half the night pondering insignificant options. It wasn't until the heat of late morning, he noticed a bee flying near the leftover deer meat, and it hit him.

"Where is the nearest beehive?"

"Why?" one of the children asked.

"I need beeswax and lots of it."

The blacksmith shared his revelation with Jib, and they were taken to a nearby meadow by the child where a dead tree held a hive. The bees were swarming, hundreds of them, and both men shook their heads.

"Have you ever done this before?" Jib asked.

"Never, how about you?"

"No, not like this, but I've felt their sting."

"Me too, but usually, it's only one sting at a time. Going after the hive isn't my idea of fun."

"Do you want to draw sticks?"

"Just the two of us?"

"Not a chance. Our odds would improve dramatically if we all draw, don't you think?"

"Perfect, that works for me."

Aiden selected seven pieces of dried stick, breaking them into various lengths. Jib called the rest of the party together, showed them the hive, and explained the need. None looked too excited about their prospects after watching the swarm hovering around the topless tree.

"Each one of us has the same chance to prove their manhood with this act of courage," Aiden said, jokingly.

His comment delivered uncomfortable laughter as each drew their own fate. The strategy served Jib and Aiden well as Dak was the unlucky soul holding the short stick. He was the youngest, tallest, and the silent one of the group until now.

"You expect me to stick my hand in that hive?"

"That's how it's done," Jib replied.

"I don't think so. There has to be another way."

"It's the only way."

"You're telling me you'd stick your hand in that hive to find honeycomb."

"I don't have to. I didn't draw the short stick."

"Dak, it's not that bad, if you piss on your hands, they won't sting you."

"You expect me to believe that, Hondo?"

"I'm only trying to help."

"Then you do it."

"I didn't draw the short stick either. We don't have all day. Be the man and get to it."

Reluctantly, Dak wrapped cloth around his head, after cutting eyeholes and gradually approached the tree, one step at a time. He kept looking back at the long sticks, who were following his progress, and once he was close enough, pissed on his hands. Hondo restrained a humorous outburst as did the others, all smirking in silence.

Arriving at the tree, the bees continued to swarm, but didn't attack. Their lack of aggression made Dak feel more comfortable and confident in his task. He slowly slid his hand inside, feeling around for the honeycomb. Hondo realized his piss sarcasm was actually working. No one else knew any different; they would think him clever and wise, which he'd proudly take credit for in his scheme.

Little by little, Dak removed his hand, a large chunk of honeycomb in his grasp. The bees became more agitated, but still hadn't stung the thief. When he ran, they followed, causing everyone else to scatter. Once he passed by his friends, he dropped the wax and began waving his arms and slapping his chest as he sprinted for the river with bees in his shirt. When the swarm dispersed, Aiden collected the comb and headed toward the water's edge where Dak stood, splashing and frantically trying to remove his shirt.

"You did that quite well. Don't forget to wash your hands," Hondo announced to all in earshot.
"It worked, and that's all I care about. I should have pissed on my shirt too."
"How many times were you stung?"
"Seven, I think."
"Some people die when they're stung that many times."
"You're kidding, right?"
"Not for a moment. It's like a snakebite."
"Like an asp."
"No, it takes longer. The poison isn't as potent."
"So what do I do?"
"Let me know if you have trouble breathing."
"And how long will that take?"
"You'll know soon enough."

The likelihood or possibility of his own demise left Dak stressed and fidgety. One child showed him how to apply mudpacks to beestings and reduce the swelling and pain, which eased his distress somewhat. Finally, after an hour, he realized the danger had passed. It was time to boast of his success.

One of the women heated the comb enough to remove as much honey as she could before returning it to Aiden. He cut the soft wax into smaller pieces and kept it warm and pliable near the fire. Jib retrieved the second hindquarter from the river and put it on the spit. After roasting a couple hours, he carved thin slices of venison and placed them on the hot rocks to draw out more moisture.

With six hours of daylight and five days travel to reach the great rock, they collected the wax and dried meat and said their farewells to the helpful village. Jib was convinced they could follow the river to the mountains where they could cross over to the sea. From there, the Egyptians could find a boat to take them home and Aiden, transport to continue his quest. All agreed there was no other alternative.

The next four days were uneventful. They made good time and never found the other mobile village. Their last camp before the great rock was along the river shallows with fallen trees and submerged rocks. It was a perfect place to catch a fish dinner. Three arrows and a little wading was all it took. While they sat around the campfire, they noticed two fires burning on the other side of the river. The river was still too wide and the current too swift to cross, but the sentry kept watch on the hostiles as they surely were doing the same.

When morning came, Aiden reheated the wax, and they inserted the soft material in their ears. This leg of the expedition would be challenging since none would be able to hear each other or any approaching danger. It was a strange sensation that would require extreme caution, eye contact, and hand signals. While they broke camp, they spotted the hostiles doing the same and, as they began moving upriver, realized they were being paced by the other side. It was evident they wanted themselves to be seen with numbers significant enough to intimidate.

For the remainder of the afternoon, their movement was mirrored stride for stride. In the coming days, the river would become narrower and a potential crossing more imminent. Avoiding another conflict was vital, and separation from the river could be in their future. When and where would depend on the river itself.

Finally, the rock wall came into view where the bend shifted the waters' course to the south. It was a massively flat outcrop, hundreds of feet high. The closer they drew, the more they contemplated the hypnotic effects of the siren's song, each life depending on the craft of a bee. In silence, the party reached the trailhead at the base of the rock, which would lead them up and around the monument.

Caves were visible near the waters' edge, but no sign of the siren was apparent. One last glance across the river and her enchantment became truth. Two men jumped in the river and tried swimming across, but the current was carrying them away from her spell. So entranced, the two continued to try and reach their call to the rock until both sank out of sight. Overpowering reactions to their plight were spoken but fell on deaf ears as they moved on.

The trailhead wrapped around the rock, rather than over, gradually elevating as it progressed. The animal-worn path had a fairly steep incline on the left and decline on the right, both enveloped in the shadows of the canopy. The travel wasn't difficult and the footing was sure as long as they hugged the incline side of their course.

Nearing the halfway point, Jib noticed the group was one man short. The column came to an abrupt halt as he shared his revelation by holding up six fingers. It was Dak, the last in their chain, who was missing. They began working back down the trail, fearing the worst. After a short search, they found evidence of something or someone sliding down the decline.

Jib carefully worked his way down the bank, using the trees and roots to keep his footing. Branches were broken and the dirt disturbed, but no Dak. He thought about yelling out his name, but with wax in his ears, he'd never hear the call. Jib began climbing back up, knowing they would have to go farther down the trail to reunite. On his way up, he stumbled onto one thing he wish he hadn't, a piece of wax. Once back at the path, he shared his evidence with the others and then stuffed the wax in his pocket.

They knew what they had to do, but it would've been much easier if they could talk about it first. The siren surely had Dak under her bewitching spell, and their challenge was figuring out how to liberate him if that was even possible. The caves belonged to Lorelei and the Egyptian belonged to her. The siren would do everything in her power to keep his soul and seize theirs too.

Arriving back at the trailhead and standing on the riverbank, they saw entrances of two caves partially concealed by branches and vines. Both had water rippling through the openings and could only be reached by swimming. Aiden and Hondo used hand signals to tell the others they would be the ones to attempt the rescue. Jib was the only one who disagreed, wanting to go himself, but Hondo convinced him to stay behind and took the piece of wax with him.

The two rescuers eased themselves into the water and slowly paddled toward the caves. The element of surprise would require complete silence, and with wax in their ears, they couldn't be sure how quiet they really were. At the mouth of the caves, both entered the one closest to the shore first. It was the smaller of the two with shallower water. After they were a few feet in the cave, the two could wade; water was shoulder-high and declining with each step.

They reached a ledge wide enough to walk, but chose to remain on their current course. Ahead, torches flickered, illuminating a large cavern. Both kept minimal profiles, only their heads detectable as wade became a crawl. When Hondo's hand bumped something foreign, he raised his find to the surface and tapped Aiden on the shoulder. It was a human leg bone. The blacksmith, in turn, displayed a skull. Each was the remains of an unfortunate victim.

Ahead, more bones were strewn about the cavern floor, some in small piles and one larger one, consisting of skulls. At least a hundred bewitched fatalities of Lorelei's spell lay in disarray. Both wondered how long her prey could survive before reaching their demise, but couldn't communicate their thoughts. Men were her toys to manipulate and control for as long or as short as she could. Was it possible that Dak was already dead?

The two slowly and carefully crept out of the water and backed against the cave wall, advancing through deliberate measures. The cavern was much deeper then they originally thought, and as they progressed, torches became fewer and the grotto darker. The only secrets revealed were more bones. Somewhere, there was access to the second cave, but going deeper didn't seem prudent, so they returned to the opening with the same degree of caution.

Hondo signaled those on the beach to let them know he and the blacksmith were about to enter the other cave, just in case they were needed for some reason. Jib was relieved to see both men were still unharmed.

Entering the second opening was similar to the first except for no bones and more torches. There was an awful smell that penetrated their nostrils and turned their stomachs. Leaning against the right wall were two rotting human carcasses, each at a different level of deterioration. It appeared the cave had at least three separated compartments with a fire burning in the second.

As they eased forward, shadows danced off the farthest wall. It was two figures melted into one, like the two were struggling or dancing with each other. They moved quickly toward the thrashing motions, staying presumably silent and peeked into the chamber. The figures still weren't visible, except for the shadows, but most of the room was. A large golden harp centered the space, surrounded by various pieces of elaborate wood and vine furniture. Grand mirrors were mounted on separate walls to validate Lorelei's enchanting vanity.

Hondo and Aiden looked at each other with amazement and prepared to rush into the room. No sooner had they gained entry, their progress came to a standstill. The shadows became life forms. The two weren't fighting, and they weren't dancing. The huntress was fucking her prey with a passionate torture and taunting. Their naked bodies were tangled upon a wooden vine-tied bed, complete with a canopy supporting a gray owl.

The Egyptian and blacksmith were awestruck by the revelations of the room. Their union was a violent sexual eruption, yet Dak displayed no signs of pain, only displays of extreme pleasure. Neither rescuer had seen anything like it in their lives. The winged siren held the dominant position as Dak grasped her breasts. It appeared her enchantment wasn't all bad as Dak was receiving the fuck of his life and might have the chance to live to tell about it.

If they were going rescue their friend, it was now while Lorelei was distracted. Dak could see their approach, but was too preoccupied to respond as if in a trance. Hondo took a piece of rope and quickly wrapped it around her neck, pulling her backward toward him. Aiden, with wax in hand, found Dak's empty ear and pushed the soft compound down the canal. The reaction was almost immediate as his sweat-covered body tried to catch its breath and struggled to lift him to his feet.

The siren thrashed about, attempting to flap her wings, in a desperate endeavor to escape the rope that Hondo had secured around her neck. His grasp was firm and unyielding until all three were behind her. Aiden pulled one of her feathers as he passed, but wasn't sure why he reacted so at the time. Hondo released the rope and pushed the siren back on the bed as the three men ran to escape the cave, never looking back.

When the water was deep enough, they dove in, swimming like they were in a race. Once they reached the shallows of the shore, they were pulled out of the water and laid on the grass for mere seconds to catch their breath. Getting to their feet and still breathing hard, their focus returned to the image of the caves. Lorelei never made her appearance, and they wondered if daylight may have played a factor.

Rhinegold Maidens

Jib motioned to leave, and the group made a hasty departure. Once they reached the farthest advancement of their prior travels, the leader halted for a timely break. Hondo thought about what he'd witnessed and wondered what it would feel like to experience the enchantment of Lorelei's call. If they were securely tied to a tree, each one of them could hear her song and feel its seduction.

He thought it was a great idea to satisfy his curiosity and decided to make it happen. Each one took a turn at the tree, except Dak, who already had more than he could handle. All six heard the harp and felt the bewitching power of her beautiful yet sad song. Every one of the tortured souls fought to free themselves and begged for their release to pursue her. The anguish was maddening and the experience mind-altering.

At the castle, Princess Ariana received word through her father that seven bodies had washed up on the beach, all drowning victims. She sat in the garden and cried, concerned about Aiden and thankful he wasn't one of the seven. She held out hope that all was well and he would return to claim her love. Scota also heard the news and was equally grateful about her cousin. Both women suffered through the hot days and long nights, tossing and dreaming about the fate of those they love.

The wizard had his visions too. His were more detailed and accurate than the others. He knew of the dangers taking place and how many were actively pursuing the feather. Twenty-seven of the original thirty-eight were still alive, but he kept what he knew to himself and prayed his visions didn't reveal Aiden's demise, for he wouldn't be able to keep that kind of secret from the princess.

Jib continued the march until he was reasonably sure the siren's song would have no effect. Hondo and Aiden held his arms while Dak took the wax from his right ear. The music had no impact, and they all removed their wax. It was a relief to hear all their voices again. There was much to converse, so they set an early camp, collected firewood, and lit the fire of chat initiated by Jib.

"So, Dak, give us an account of your encounter with the siren."

"It was incredible. I lost my footing and tumbled over the bank, losing my wax in the process. After that, the song hypnotized my brain to believe I had to return to her cave. I couldn't stop myself, she was calling my name."

"What happened when you got there?"

"She stopped singing and removed my wet clothes."

"And then?"

"She acted like my penis was hers. I thought she was going to suck my brains out. It was the first time I ever felt the power of a woman's lips, and her beauty was indescribable. I wanted her essence, every inch of her body."

"We caught your sexual exploits in the act," Aiden admitted. "You looked over the edge."

"I couldn't stop. I'd already had two orgasms, and I can't begin to tell you how many she had, except they were multiple."

"She was fucking you to death, Dak, literally. If we hadn't got there when we did, you'd be dead, and her obsession with sex wouldn't have stopped until you were," Hondo declared.

"It didn't feel like I would die. It was the most terrific sensation of my life."

"By the end of the day, you'd have been just another rotting corpse."

"Then thank you for saving me from my hour of bliss, but I'll never be able to forget it for the rest of my life, and I'm sure no other woman will be able to take me anywhere near the same level of ecstasy."

"That is a fact, but Lorelei is a witch without a heart. Don't underestimate the powers of the heart and love. Lorelei doesn't love, she destroys."

Conversation around the campfire continued for some time. Lorelei's enchantment was on each of their minds after each had been tied to a tree. They all had the same visions of her beauty and sexual torment, but the most surprising revelation was she called each of them by name, giving her power over men a deeper, more personal measure.

The fires across the river were visible again. They too had been touched by the siren and had some way to counter the effect of her song, except for the two, who never reached the caves. They persisted in shadowing Aiden's party upriver, for some unknown reason. Were they so aggressive in nature that they had nothing else to do?

Jib decided they wouldn't light a fire for the next few nights and see if the adversary fires kept burning. With some luck, they might think they had traveled inland and discontinue moving east. Their movements would also involve leaving the river's edge so they couldn't be viewed from the opposite shore during daylight. Both were worth a try.

Jib's idea of becoming invisible began the following morning. Their progress was slowed dramatically since they had to blaze their own trail through the woodland. Keeping the sounds of the river within earshot would keep them on course. By day's end, fires still burned on a southeastern heading. The same was true on the second night as well.

Jib considered that maybe it didn't matter whether they could be seen or not. With the river turning to rapids, the hostiles could be looking for a reasonable place to cross or maybe they already knew where the channel was the shallowest. If that were true and chances were they knew the river better than he did, they were at risk. The danger they faced couldn't be ignored. They would have to leave the river, for now, and move much farther inland than they had planned.

The next day, they traveled north, reaching the foothills, which they ascended. From the rolling summits, they could view the river valley below and monitor the movements of their rivals. Fires were still detectable from the elevated perch and assured that distance between the two could be measured by at least a day.

The panorama from the hilltops was remarkable, including a view of the ocean, although faint. The river curved back to the east and into a valley of the foothills. From their outlook, the distant snowcapped mountains came into view. They were the door to the inland sea and the destination that would set their route.

At the next encampment, the bonfires of their pursuers had found their way to the opposite shore. The crossing proved the Egyptian's theory was correct. He was sure, once they pick up his tracks, they would follow. If Bird was right about the nature of the horde, they would be persistent in their pursuit and, by now, were probably pissed. Their threat and intimidation had worked, but the surprise crossing and strike had not.

Jib's military training had saved their lives, and he continued to think like a soldier. He was good at outthinking his opponent; he'd done it before, although this time was a totally different situation. He had a plan and called everyone together to share his thoughts.

"Beautiful view, isn't it?"

"Yes."

"You all know, they are persistent and not going away." He pointed toward the valley. "We have to resort to drastic action."

"I hope by drastic, you don't mean fight?" Dak reacted to the comment.

"No, of course not, but we can continue to outsmart them."

"How, exactly?" Aiden asked.

"We've done it so far. Ask yourselves, what would they least expect?"

They looked at each other, but not one of them answered.

"We have to cross the river. They would never anticipate that move. It's the only way to avoid confrontation."

"What happens after we cross the river? They live on that side. Where there are some, there could be many."

"True, but I believe their villages are farther to the west and chances of encountering another party is slim at best."

The consensus was unanimous, but none looked forward to going back down the mountains. It was still daylight when they reached the bank of the river and the swift rapids. The water spanned half the distance that it had two days earlier. There were plenty of places to cross, using the rocks and downed trees, as long as they weren't careless. If any were swept downstream, they might end up back in the grasp of Lorelei and certain death.

Hondo was the first to traverse the rapids with a rope tied around his waist. The others observed his progress as he navigated the wet logs and slick rocks, waiting for him to reach the opposite side and scout the area for any unwelcome raiders. Once he was assured it was safe, he untied the rope and Jib pulled it back across. All tied together, the rest followed his path.

Dak seemed to be a victim of his own destiny, losing his footing on the slick rocks and getting caught in the current. His weight and the driving force of the rapids caused a second to falter and then a third. Only Dak was being pulled by the driving force of the water, but if they didn't react and regroup, they would all be swept away. Jib and Aiden both anchored themselves in the rocks to stabilize the other three. It took a few minutes, especially since Dak had to be reeled in, but it was accomplished with only minor scratches.

"Dak, are you really such an oaf?" Jib asked in disgust.

"No, just my bad luck."

"Then why are you the only one having this *BAD LUCK?*"

Dak held a guilty expression and appeared to be searching for an answer.

"It's time you changed your *LUCK* for the good of us all. We can't afford any more accidents that put us at risk."

Dak nodded his head in affirmation, and they renewed their trek north. The moon generated enough light to allow the seven to follow the river after dark and put more distance behind them. They didn't see any more fires after that.

When they reached the foothills once again from the southern side, the river twisted up the valley like a snake. For the first time, the water cascaded over rocks and wood debris. From here, they would begin an ascent that would be ongoing for days; the pace would be demanding and slowed.

Staying close to the river was difficult at times, due to the terrain. They left the foothills behind and scaled the first of many lower mountains until reaching a small hidden lake encompassed by a lush meadow. The time for a hot meal was long overdue, and a campfire could be lit again. Several varieties of birds were here for the summer, while for others, it was their natural habitat. Fowl over the fire was the perfect way to satisfy their hunger and the hunt began.

The meal of pigeon, grouse, and one goose was filling yet messy. Instead of washing their hands, they chose to go swimming in the ice-cold water. The dip was refreshing, but short-lived due to their limbs growing numb and skin turning blue. They stood naked around the fire, warming their skin and improving their circulation. They had earned a good night's sleep, and even though it seemed safe, they posted a sentry throughout the night.

Atum was the last Egyptian to stand watch. The early daybreak was so peaceful with a light fog hovering over the lake and dew clinging to the grass. The distinct sounds of the native creatures echoed, some in conversation. A variety of fauna came visiting the shore to satisfy their morning thirst, and an entire herd of deer with fawns in tow. Nature was a beautiful thing, pure and magical.

He was so mesmerized by the panorama; he was unaware of a creeping danger that loomed much closer. Suddenly, more sensed than heard, he spun around to meet a deadly prospect.

A muscular brown bear, standing on its hind legs, was less than ten feet away and ready to have him for breakfast.

"*BEAR!*"

The desperate scream had everyone scrambling to gather themselves upright and secure a weapon. The right claw swiped through the air, striking Atum across his left cheek, instantly knocking the Egyptian to the ground. The bear lunged downward, exposing its gaping jaws and massive fangs. The teeth ripped through his left shoulder, causing excruciating pain, as he struggled frantically to escape

The assault was met by Aiden's sword triggering a defensive reaction in his direction. The bear took a second swipe at Atum as it rose to smack the sword out of the blacksmith's hand. Without hesitation, he instantly drew his daggers, burying the first in the neck and the second between the front legs. He was taken down in a second, but the bear fell on top motionless before it could inflict any damage. The animal was so heavy; he could barely breathe until the weight shifted as the bear was rolled over. Three arrows were buried deep; one passed through the neck and two in the chest.

"*CRAP*, I thought I was a goner."

Aiden got to his feet, towered over the beast, and pulled out his daggers. It was the second time they had tasted blood and wouldn't be the last. He turned to face the fallen comrade, who was already receiving aid. His cheek bore a disfiguring blow, but the wound to the shoulder was deep and bleeding profusely as Jib attempted to slow the flow.

"We have to move him to the lake. I need the cold water to help coagulate the blood and clean the wounds."

Together, they moved him to a blanket and carried him to the waters' edge. Jib took his shirt and dipped it in the cold water, saturating the cloth and laying it across the shoulder. Another cloth was wet and applied to the facial wounds. Hondo gave Aiden the look, and he knew Atum's prospects were severe. Jib was doing everything physically possible to address his critical needs, but even he realized the seriousness of the situation. If the injuries weren't fatal, it would still take weeks before Atum would be able to travel.

He was carried back to the campsite and made as comfortable as they could, given the certainty he faced. Jib and Hondo both took turns tending to their friend for hours while Aiden and Dak skinned the bear and stretched the hide over a makeshift frame to dry by the fire. The blacksmith also removed the claws and teeth to make a necklace sometime during his journey. It was a long day; the Egyptian fighting to overcome his devastation. His struggle ended under a blanket of stars and a disturbing silence from his comrades.

No one wanted to talk, whether the time wasn't right or they didn't know what to say. None slept and the silence continued until dawn. The hush was finally broken by their remorseful leader.

"He was a good man. I can't bear the thought of telling his family. This was only supposed to be a simple voyage, not a death march, and we still have so far to go. How many more will we lose?"

"I'm so sorry. This is all my fault."

"It's nobody's fault, Aiden, it's just the reality we face. We can't control our own destiny or anyone else's. Fate is in the hands of the gods."

"The quest still makes me responsible."

"No, none of us could control this deadly outcome, and this adventure was something we all looked forward to. It's just not the adventure we expected."

Atum was buried at the base of a giant oak with Jib saying a few words over his grave before breaking camp and continuing east. It was a somber ascent, lasting all day. They had lost two of their own so far, and nothing more was said until they reached a suitable camp.

The site had a waterfall that fed a stream flowing to the rapids below. The snowcapped peaks were about three days away, depending on the difficulty involved in finding a reasonable route to the other side. Aiden knew it would be freezing once they hit the high snow, so he cut the hide into three pieces and made insulated coats. The others were impressed by his craftiness.

"There are six of us and only three jackets. It's only fair we draw sticks. The losers get the winners' extra clothes for additional warmth, agreed?"

Everyone approved the democratic approach. Hondo gathered the twigs and broke them into varying size. Aiden was the last to draw and held the longest piece. Dak and Jib also won a hide.

"I think my luck has finally changed," Dak said with a broad smile.

"Maybe, but don't spend all your luck in one place. It could be essential you save some for later," Jib quipped.

"I'm feeling pretty lucky myself," Aiden responded.

"Luck isn't destiny or fate, it's luck. Think of it more in terms of an accidental fluke. Your blessing can change with the snap of your fingers."

It was slight humor, all around, which was sorely needed to release the built-up stress of the last two days. Everyone was aware of the danger in losing focus. Every day had to be taken seriously; it wasn't a game of chance. Becoming too relaxed could cost another member of the group his life. It was a war of survival, and they had to behave like soldiers. There was no future in a weak link or opportunity in a costly mistake.

Aiden cleaned his daggers in the creek. He should have cleaned them after the bear was killed, but he didn't. It was expected that a man clean the blood from a blade after battle to maintain the quality of a sharp edge, but the distractions of the incident diverted his concentration.

The following afternoon, they happened across another lake, also surrounded by a grove and meadow of yellow flowers. This one was fed by twin waterfalls that backwashed to form a reasonably large pond between them, bordered with large smooth rocks. The waters were inviting, and with the spray rising from the falls, it cast a magical eminence.

The lake was a timely find as they reached the base of the high mountains. A good rest would prepare them for the difficult assault over the next couple days. Hot and sweaty, they stripped down and bathed beneath the falls and immersed their bodies in the serenity of the pool. After cleansing their bodies, they washed their clothes and laid them on the rocks before stretching out in the meadow to let the sun parch their skin.

While some took a nap, others just relaxed in a face up or down prone position until they were dry. Aiden was the first to rise from the grass and retrieve his clothes, but they were gone, all gone, every stitch to the man. He made quick glances in every direction, which revealed nothing out of the ordinary. He was stymied by the strange theft.

"*HEY!* Our clothes have disappeared."

The announcement brought everyone to their feet and assembled them around the rocks. Each was perplexed with the loss and searched the surrounding area in their nakedness without a clue.

"Someone's been here. Did anyone see or hear anything unusual?" Jib asked.

"I didn't and I was awake the whole time," Aiden replied. "Who would want to steal our clothes, for what purpose?"

"Someone is playing tricks on us. If it was one of you, tell me now."

They all shook their heads with a sense of disgust that Jib would pose such theft.

"*WE WANT OUR CLOTHES BACK, RIGHT NOW!*" Dak shouted to the world.

No response was forthcoming with the exception of his own faint echo. Frustrated, Jib gathered them in the middle of the grove and posted a lookout to focus on nothing but the pond in hopes someone or something would reveal itself. The more time that passed, the colder it got, and the heat of the concealed fire became more critical as did the bear hides.

The moonlit night cast a golden sheen on the lake and pool as the plummeting splatter of the waterfalls mimicked each other in a hypnotic rhythm. It was Dak's watch; he rubbed his eyes and slapped himself on the cheek, trying to sustain his concentration when he noticed something moving near the pool. The image was vague, so he crept through the trees from one to another to get a better look. The figure became two, then three, detailed enough to be females. He observed them frolicking in the pool for a few moments and then returned to alert the others.

In the hope of not making noise that would startle or disperse the women, he woke up the sleeping travelers, one at a time, with a soft whisper. Quiet was the word as they inched ever closer to a view of the thieves.

"Not more beautiful and seductive women. I wonder how dangerous THEY are," Dak posed.

"And this time there's three of them," Aiden added.

"None of us are under the influence of a spell for now, and they aren't singing," Hondo pointed out.

"Well, something's amiss, but I don't know what. Women this isolated and stealing our clothes must have some purpose that's hard to reason. We have to assume they possess some type of dominance over us," Jib warned.

The women caressed their own bodies and each other's, too, in a seductive dance that finally broke into song. The men raised their hands to plug both ears in a defensive motion, realizing instantly that the song had no enchanting effect.

"That's reassuring," Aiden said with a sigh of relief as he unplugged his ears.

"Yeah, but what else can we expect?"

"A good show. Maybe their sexual prowess is for our benefit."

"What makes you say that?"

"Because they're hugging, kissing, and we've lost our clothes. I'm sure they know we're naked and watching every seducing move they make. It's like they're sending us an invitation to join them."

"I'll volunteer to prove your point," Dak responded enthusiastically.

"Haven't you had enough already? What's wrong with you? Maybe someone else wants to step forward for the good of us all."

"Not me, I have a princess that's waiting. If I don't listen to my heart, then I've forgotten the purpose of my quest and might as well go home."

"Seriously, indulging in such senseless behavior without knowing the risk is foolish. Despite their allure, they remain adversaries who've stolen our garments. They are lovely and enticing, but let's see how they respond to a bow or a blade."

The naked men approached, armed, but showing no force until the very last moment. One of the women instantly changed herself into an owl and flew to the nearby trees. A second took the form of a frog, slipping between the rocks that surrounded the pool. The men were astonished by the spontaneous transformations except for Jib.

"If you change form, you will surely die," Jib told the third nymph with a blade at her throat.

"Please don't. I will remain as I am."

"And who are you?"

"My name is Flosshilde. The eldest of three Rhinegold Maidens."

"You're more than mere maidens."

"Nymphs, shape-shifters as you can see."

"We can see that, but why did you steal our clothes?"

"Men don't pass this way every day. We have needs and so do they. Fulfilling their fantasy is the essence of our being. We long for the splendor of masculine dominance and fortitude."

"We only want what's ours, returned."

"That is a strange reaction to such a passionate surrender. Willpower is an unusual response to erotic lust."

"For you, I'm sure. When do we get our clothes?"

"I will retrieve them now if you like."

"We like, but not you. Send one of the others."

The frog became a woman again, passing through the waterfall and exiting with a bundle in her arms. One at a time, they claimed their threads and clad their nakedness.

"We will leave you as you are, but I ask your word that you won't take some form that will cause us harm in any way."

"Promise, but we ask something from you in return."

"What could you possibly need from us besides a penis?"

"As Rhinegold Maidens, we were guardians of precious treasures that were ours to protect and defend. The treasure was stolen from us by a dwarf named Alberich while he was invisible, infuriating Lilith and the gods. The dwarf made a ring from the gold, and our reputations are affronted until the ring is found and returned to the guardians."

"Why would he risk their wrath? Was it greed?"

"Alberich is chieftain of the Nibelungen, king of the dwarfs. He's not a handsome man, but he had a strong sexual desire and wanted any one of us for his own. Even through his invisibility, which added mystic to our encounters and hid his image, we rebuked him. He cursed love out of frustration and turned into a greed monger, stealing the treasure."

"Good story, but how do you see us helping to resolve your dilemma?"

"Being the travelers that you are, there is a chance you could happen upon his cave in the mountains. His realm is an underground castle carved out of rock, but the location is elusive. If you stumble upon his grotto, you could retrieve the ring and return it to us."

"Why would you expect us to do that?"

"Because you are men of upstanding character."

"We try, but we're not perfect."

"We're not looking for perfection, but it's the imperfection of men that corrupts their souls and surrenders them weak to our nature. You maintain control of your senses and possess a level of integrity we can trust, most uncommon characteristics from those we usually encounter, you know, the selfish, indulging mortals of pleasure."

"I have a few questions before I decide. Are you nocturnal?"

"Sometimes. We enjoy the sun, but there is something erotic and powerful about the shadows of night when it comes to men's libido."

"And who is Lilith?'

"Lilith is the goddess of desire and lustful dreams. She is a seductress, a witch, a shape-shifter, and a queen in her own right. She can control women through mirrors, men with sexual pleasure, and the beast of the field with the south wind."

"She sounds wickedly powerful."

"She can be the woman of your dreams, which never lasts beyond her immediate needs, or your most appalling and dreadful nightmare from which there is no escape."

"And where can she be found?"

"Wherever or whenever she wants to be found, but usually she inhabits the waters of life and the depths of hell."

Aiden's ears caught the reference to the waters of life. Scota had mentioned it with reference to the phoenix and the healing powers the water itself. He had to ask.

"Do you have knowledge of the phoenix and the water of life?"

"I do, but why do you ask?"

"Because I'm on a quest for its feather."

"That's an undertaking not likely to succeed. A quest for the phoenix or the water of life could be a quest for Lilith and certain death."

"Do you know where to find them?"

"Their location is not for us to know, both are shrouded in secrecy."

"By Lilith?"

"Yes, but I wouldn't be looking for her if I were you."

"Can you describe her appearance for me?"

"There are two portrayals. Her natural image is one of eternal beauty with pale skin, red rose lips, and golden hair. The curves of her body and perfect breasts are beyond rebuff by any man or woman alike. There is no refusing the allure of her hypnotic charm or advances."

"And what of her unnatural side?"

"As a shape-shifter, she can take any form she wants. She prefers nocturnal varieties, particularly the screech owl and vampire bat. It's said she has drank the blood of her victims.

As a goddess of the night, she strives to steal the souls of young children while they sleep.

"She is capable of changing her image to male, if she so chooses or your best friend, lover, or spouse. That's why she's never refused, no is not an option with her. Her reactions can be vicious and unforgiving or manipulative and granting, it all depends on the whim of her motivation and control. She can also wipe your mind clean of her encounter. We are creatures of her realm as is Lorelei, the siren, who lives in the caves downriver. How is it that you managed to avoid the allure of her seductive song?"

"We've encountered the siren and were fortunate to get out with our lives."

"Lucky for you, but unlucky for her. Escaping her bewitchment brings about her own death unless Lilith, as she did with us, forgives Lorelei for her failure to serve a higher purpose."

"I thank you for being receptive to our questions," Jib said, expressing gratitude. "We will be sympathetic to your dilemma and perceptive in our travels. It is possible we might stumble on Alberich's cave along our road, but we won't go out of our way to search for it."

"Agreed, thank you for being honorable."

"Thank you for your honesty and returning our clothes."

Edric's Magic

Returning to the campsite, Hondo covered their retreat. They packed up all their goods and gave the maidens one last look before they started their climb. The nymphs were back to their frolic and song as if nothing prior had occurred, but then, there was nothing normal about any of the women that had crossed their path so far.

They began to scale the mountains while it was still dark. The moonlight provided enough brightness to see the trail, and they wanted to put some distance between them and the maidens. The climb was made easier while the air was so cool. The higher they ascended, the steeper it got until they were forced to stop and to tether each other for their own safety.

Reaching the first peak exposed a deep valley carved by the river and a remote rope bridge spanning the gorge. They hoped the rope wasn't rotten, or it would be a long way to fall. They would know the condition soon enough and judge if it was safe to cross. It took another hour to reach the bridge and time to inspect its status. The drop was a good two hundred feet to the rocks below, and they decided their best action was to remain tied to one another.

The bridge itself was a series of ropes tied into knots, traversing the river in the shape of a V. None had ever crossed a rope bridge before, so there was a little apprehension tugging at their confidence. Footing and balance would be critical to the sluggish crossing if they wanted to control the swing of the rope. Each made sure all their gear and weapons were secure and took several deep breaths in preparation of the challenge that lay ahead.

Hondo took the lead and set the pace. Once all were underway, the rope began to sway slightly, creating a sense of weightlessness. They couldn't help but look down, which only intensified the terror that none would admit, and the closer they got to the halfway point, the stronger the wind. It got so bad at one point, they came to a complete stop, in hopes the freak gusts would die down. To make matters worse, it began to rain with the force of needles to their skin.

With the escalating wind, the bridge was caught in a dramatic free swing, making some sick to their stomach. Aiden, again, was the first to puke, but not the last. The party entwined their arms and legs in the vertical ropes of the bridge for stability, knowing they would be anchored there until the breeze died down and the bridge steadied.

They were immobile for so long, they began to question the decision to cross the bridge in the first place, wondering if they should go back instead of forward. They were stuck on a swinging bridge they hoped wouldn't snap under the added weight and pressure to the rope. Were there powers unseen that marked their travels? All they could do was hang on and wait and wait and wait.

The group was stranded for more than an hour when the wind finally began to subside and none too soon. Their grasps were so tight that fingers were numb and feeling was fleeting. When the sway seemed manageable, Hondo got to his feet and continued the last segment of the traverse at a more hurried pace. All they wanted to do was get off the rope and on the land before the gusts returned.

Once they all reached the other side of the bridge, they collapsed with exhaustion, relieved to be alive. It took a while to regroup and restore the circulation to their limbs, but once they were all breathing normally and able to walk without feeling gimpy, they started out again, happy to leave the bridge behind them.

A short distance up the trail was an undersized cave, partially hidden by bushes. It looked the right size for a dwarf, so Jib and Aiden decided to check it out. Both had to bend over to clear the entrance, but once inside, it proved to be uninhabited for some time. There were animal drawings on the walls, but no fresh footprints, and they couldn't be sure if the cave had ever been Alberich's.

Meanwhile, Scota knocked on the oval-topped wooden door of the wizard's gatehouse. She hadn't talked to Edric since the quest had begun and knew he would be able to enlighten her. He answered her tap, dressed in a long black robe with hair and beard of white.

"Scota."

"Edric the white."

"What can I do for you?"

"You know exactly what you can do. I shouldn't have to say it."

"Come in and we'll talk."

The Egyptian princess had never been inside the gatehouse, in fact, very few had walked its floors. Flickering candles were everywhere, casting unusual shadows on the ceiling and walls. One wall had lines of glass jars containing various ingredients of powders, liquids, and herbs. She walked beside a long table below the containers with cauldrons of differing size, used for mixing and crushing. Glass containers of contrasting size and shape were scattered about along with burners to heat the alchemist's magic concoctions.

The other side of the room contained one large cauldron, positioned on the floor, along with various utensils and other odd things hanging from the wall. Mounted at its center was a great mirror with a frame of moving liquid. Scota's curiosity was drawn to the mirror first as soon as she saw it, but instead, she followed the wizard to the fireplace, taking a seat on the hearth opposite him.

"I can only imagine the magic that's been conjured up in this room."

"That's what I do, practical and prudent, as odd as it sounds. Magic is a delicate science with reckless consequence."

"Do you cast spells?"

"I can, but spells should be cast very selectively. One has to be held accountable for his actions and consider the final outcome of a spell."

"Ever had a spell go wrong?"

"I have, that's why I'm selective. Spells can cause irreparable damage in the wrong hands and can be counter spelled by another witch or wizard. I prefer those that are not easily detectable or traceable back to its creator."

"How do you keep track of your magic?"

"I make notations in my Book of Spells, although I did miss the siren episode, which could have been disastrous. Our friends had left Lorelei's caves behind them, but a misstep by Dak, caused him to return, under an enchantment spell. Lorelei had him in her grasp, but he was rescued without loss. I assumed the danger had passed, and I was mistaken, but I can't stand in front of the mirror every hour of every day."

"I've come to ask if you'd please share your visions. I realize it's an unorthodox request, but I still have family and friends that haven't returned from their voyage to the Balearic Islands and I'm concerned."

"Your request is unorthodox. It's not common practice, or even practical, for a wizard to open the door of his craft to a mortal without considering negative results."

"I understand, with respect, but you and I have consorted to create these situations of mutual benefit, involving this quest, have we not?"

"We have. If I share, I share with you alone. There are limits to what you can reveal to others. Even the king has requested details and been denied. I feed him only what he can handle and enough to satisfy his position by convincing him it would diminish my power by sharing anymore."

"My life has been surrounded in secrets, both here and in my homeland. Living with them can be demanding, but secrets are the reality by which we're judged, and truth can only be shared through trust and secrecy."

"I trust."

"Can you tell me what's happened to delay their return?"

"There is no voyage beyond the mainland. The ship was destroyed, and they're on foot, following the course of the Rhine River."

"Are they all still alive and well?"

"I hesitate to answer such fate."

"Since you hesitate, I realize casualties might exist, but please, I need to know."

"Horus has died in battle with pirates, and Atum was killed by a bear. I'm truly sorry to be the bearer of such sad news."

Scota dropped her head to meet her folded hands and catch her tears. The loss was great, but her cousin was alive and Aiden wasn't alone. She knew the revelation could have been much worse.

"Do you know where they are right now?"

"I can show you."

Edric got up and walked to the great mirror with Scota close behind. He passed his right hand across the front of the reflective glass in a circular motion, causing the liquid to become red and images to slowly appear.

"This is a one-way portal requiring a set of eyes to work. I cast a spell on a crow, giving me his eyes. The crow's been with them since the day they departed. I cast a spell of invisibility on the bird, so it could fly very close without being detected."

"Clever, I see they're in the mountains."

"The Alps, they're crossing to reach the inland sea."

"Do they still have dangers to face?"

"That's a certainty, but nothing I can visualize in the future. The mirror only reflects the present and there's a limit to how many spells can be cast in an existing realm of recipients without interfering with each other."

"Then you've cast more spells?"

"A few. Some are only temporary spells designed for a specific situation. When the Rhinegold Maidens were exposed, I became aware of knowledge they possessed, but would never willingly reveal. I cast a spell so they would give the information to Aiden freely and never know they'd divulged secrets about their own goddess."

"How would that benefit Aiden?"

"It would prepare him for his encounter with Lilith, the queen of the dark and a witch in her own right. Her powers are far greater than mine, but she won't be able to cancel a spell without knowing its origin. That doesn't mean she can't counter my spell. I cast a spell so Aiden knows what she looks like, even if she takes another form. He will see her for who she really is."

"Can she trace a spell back to you?"

"Only if she has relevant information. It will be interesting to see how Lilith reacts when she finds out Aiden is spelled, and she is unable to change to an alter form without detection."

"She's a shape-shifter?"

"The best there is and so much more. When Alberich, the dwarf king, stole the gold that the maidens were charged with guarding and made it into a ring, I knew Lilith would resort to anything in order to get it back. I cast two spells. The first made the ring invisible to her eyes and the second made the dwarf visible to Aiden's. He will be drawn to find it, although Aiden won't know where it is until he's within the reach of the spell. With the ring in his possession, he will have the ability to barter with Lilith for the phoenix feather."

"Does the dwarf pose any threat?"

"He might think so, but his magic is just trickery, and I've given Aiden the vision to see through it."

"You're a clever man and the white hair?"

"The snow of the Alps. Crossing won't be easy. It's the most physically demanding stage of their journey."

"How much time do you spend in front of this mirror?"

"More than I should, but still not enough."

"I'd like one of these to take home with me."

"With your beauty, you don't need a mirror."

"Thank you, but all women need a mirror, even if they don't know why or have none."

"There's something else."

"About the quest?"

"No, it's much closer to home. Let me show you."

The wizard walked to the floor cauldron, which was filled with a green liquid, only inches from the top.

"What I'm about to show you is a future event. I'm able to view the incident because it's within my sphere of influence. The outcome can be changed by an action that precedes it."

"Now you have me worried."

"No need to worry, just heed the warning and do what you have to, avoiding the aftermath."

"Aftermath doesn't sound good. I'm not sure I like the context of that word. Now you've got me more worried than I was before."

"I'm sorry, but it can't be helped. There is reason to be concerned, but the outcome is controllable."

Edric passed his hand over the cauldron, creating a ripple moving out from its center and dispersing into a vision of smoke, fire, and death. It took a second for the princess to focus on the detail before realizing the hamlet that was burning was her own.

"How could this happen?"

"It's the same pirates that destroyed Jib's boat. The Nordic explorations have been sailing farther south and will venture close enough to our shores to discover your village and sack it."

Scota watched as the horrifying vision played out, depicting the demise of herself and her husband, but sparing her children into slavery.

"We have to relocate."

"You do and I know you don't want to, but there's no other choice. You have to move north to the farthest point of the island. Few live there, and it will give you a future you deserve."

She nodded her head and agreed, but Edric could see her emotional frustration was devastating.

"There is good news."

"What would that possibly be?"

"The land you settle will support generations of your people and be named Scotland, in your honor."

"Well, that is something, isn't it? My very own country. I didn't leave Egypt for that."

"You won't see it happen in your lifetime, but your children will live to see the tribute bestowed to honor your life."

"How soon before we have to make this move?"

"Soon, without hesitation, I'm sorry to say. I will sorely miss our friendship and collaboration."

Scota sat and leaned back against the stone wall, staring at the ceiling for a time before taking to her feet.

"I'm going to do something you abhor, but allow me this one thing."

The princess put her arms around the wizard and gave him a lasting hug. He graciously acknowledged by returning the gesture, despite his no-touch rule.

"I will miss you and thank you for all you have shared."

"The king and Ariana know nothing of my magic spells or the details of the quest. I won't reveal anything to arouse needless worry unless I have no other choice."

"I understand, but at some point, Ariana needs to know, doesn't she?"

"I will feed her curiosity with information from time to time, but I won't share the mirror or cauldron. She'd be so emotional, she'd never leave."

"I wouldn't want to leave either and that's just what you've told me to do. In fact, I think it's time for me to go now. I have so much to do."

With a forced smile, Scota took her leave, thanked the wizard once again, and prepared to deliver the terrible news to her hamlet. Edric watched her ride away, in his own sadness, before returning to the mirror.

Hondo continued to lead the group up the trail, passing small waterfalls and springs along the way that fed a narrow summer creek. The snow in the highlands continued to melt, and the temperature edged cooler as they reached higher altitudes. The melting snow was a concern as the ice packs became more unstable. The chance of an avalanche was still real and would destroy everything in its path.

Their progress halted when they reached a divide in their path. Jib studied the two trails, choosing the one on the left, which looked more traveled, but Aiden suggested the one on the right. He sensed it was their true road, but couldn't explain why. Jib's decision was final and they continued on for some time before reaching the end of the footpath. A slide had removed any evidence it existed, leaving nothing but a sheer drop to the floor below and earth that crumbled when they tried to peer over the edge.

Aiden had been right and led their backtrack to the second option. The blacksmith wasn't sure why, but the farther they traveled up his trail, the more hesitant he became. It was an uncommon sense that left him pondering every step without reason, but the depth of his inner feelings grew ever stronger. This feeling was becoming uncomfortable and their creeping pace brought Jib to question the slow advance when Aiden finally came to a stop.

"It's the dwarf."

"Where?"

"Right there." Aiden pointed for Jib to see.

"I don't see him."

"How can you not see? He's walking the same path we are."

"Aiden, there's no one in front of us."

"But there is."

Jib asked the others if they could see the dwarf, but none could and he shared the fact with the blacksmith.

"There's something strange going on here. I know I can see him. He has a messy beard and hair of gray, a loincloth, a black cloak, and a walking stick with bones tied to it."

The dwarf turned and looked at his followers, unconcerned with their appearance since he'd used his trick of invisibility. Alberich had no idea that the wizard had given Aiden the power to see through his trick and continued on with his false sense of security.

"I can't explain this oddity, but the dwarf acts like we can't see him, and for some reason, I'm the only one who can. I think someone has cast a spell on me."

"Who could cast a spell way out here?"

"I don't know who. Maybe it's Lilith."

"Why would she cast a spell?"

"I don't know that either, unless it has something to do with the ring."

"Well then, let's follow him for a while and see if he leads us to his cave."

As Aiden tailed the dwarf, he pretended not to see him, allowing Alberich to travel with deceptive confidence. The blacksmith was sure the dwarf would lead them to his hidden cave and the prized ring. It was the only practical explanation for his gift of vision.

The dwarf turned off the primary path to a less traveled one, and Aiden could see the small cave opening, out of the corner of his eye. He continued on, leaving the dwarf a sense of security to enter his abode undetected or so he thought. Aiden stopped once everyone passed the dwarf's turn and made sure Alberich had entered his lair.

"I don't think it's a good idea all of us follow him inside since none of you can see through his invisibility. I don't know how dangerous this dwarf can be, so let's not take any chances."

"What do you have in mind?" Jib asked.

"Hondo and I will go in while the rest of you wait outside. If we need help, we'll call out. We don't know how many dwarfs inhabit the cave or whether they're invisible or not."

Everyone agreed and the duo entered the dark opening, with Aiden in the lead. The blacksmith moved quietly through the narrow limestone shaft that began snaking downward. He followed the footprints in the dusty floor as he peeked around every corner. There was a faint whiff of smoke in the air and a dim light guiding their way.

The cavern gradually became wider, revealing small stalactites and stalagmites with water dripping into small milky-white pools at their base. There was a luminescent glow from the limestone with clear crystals of various colors protruding from the walls. Finally, the vastness of the cavern was exposed with the high smoky ceiling and wide glittering walls. The scene was impressive, leaving the novice spelunkers in awe.

A distant castle fixture was carved out of the limestone walls with multiple entrances, but no movement was present. Aiden wondered where the dwarf had gone and if they would be able to get close enough to remain undetected. They both stood still and observed the site for some time before moving forward.

Once they reached the first entry of the limestone castle, Aiden made a quick glance inside. The stinky room was laden with piles of crystals, each separated by color. They both stepped inside, giving them shelter and a chance to view the cavern in more detail, remaining undetected before moving on.

Beyond the grand cavern, a shrinking shaft continued on. Two dwarfs struck remote limestone walls with their picks and, to the amazement of the spelunkers, could be observed by both. Hondo was reassured by the vision and felt more at ease with the exploration, knowing he wasn't blind to their existence. The short creatures also served to validate Aiden's visual observations. It was a relief to see what he saw.

Another dwarf stepped out of the second stone opening and walked toward the others. He was halfway there when a fourth appeared, more stout then his predecessor.

"How many do you count?" Aiden asked.
"How many do you count?"
"Four."
"Damn, I only see three."
"Okay, do you see the three at the wall?"
"I do."
"Do you see any closer than that?"
"No."
"Good, now I know which one is Alberich."

James Malcolm

The dwarf king joined the others at the wall, and Aiden signaled a move to the next door. Once inside, it was more remarkable than the last, filled with gems and precious stones of many kinds. The room had a desk with a limestone top and two rattan chairs in the back corner. On the opposite side were three cots and another smaller table. The blacksmith searched the room while Hondo kept watch, but no ring was found.

The next room they entered had a workbench full of hand tools, including hammers, chisels, and very small picks for cleaning excess stone from the gems. There was one last room to investigate, but while they were still in the workshop, Alberich began his return. The two explorers hid behind the table and waited, unsure of the dwarf's destination. His smell arrived before he did as the king grabbed a hammer and chisel before leaving again.

"That was awful," Aiden said, pinching his nose.

"I wonder how long it's been since he bathed."

"Not since his last visit to the maiden's pool would be my guess."

"That must have been some time ago, judging by the stench."

Aiden and Hondo made a dash to the final room, ducking inside. The dwarf king had reunited with the others and began knocking stones out of the limestone wall, enabling both to search the premises. The room was the largest with more elaborate furnishings. Golden figures sat on the tables and hung from the walls. This room contained precious metals not originating from the mine instead of gems. It had to be the dwarfs' stolen treasures, and if the ring wasn't here, then he must have it with him.

A medium-sized chest sat against the stone wall. It was easily carried by one man and had to be the Rhinegold treasure box. Aiden dumped the contents of the chest on the floor and looked for the ring. After a few minutes of searching, it became apparent the ring wasn't anywhere in the room. They'd hoped they wouldn't need to accost the dwarf to capture the golden band, but now, they couldn't avoid the confrontation.

They waited optimistically, weighing the possibility of facing all the dwarfs at once or the cave king alone. Neither option was to their liking. They would have preferred remaining anonymous. Since no weapons were found in any of the rooms, they assumed the dwarfs were armed. They watched the dwarfs pound away at the stone wall, sporadically dropping gems in a wooden bucket.

Finally, after some time, one of the miners walked their way. He stopped where the narrow shaft began, grabbing a cloth bag and headed to a moderate fire, dumping mushrooms in a pot, stoking the coals, and adding another piece of firewood.

Recovering the ring could take longer than they thought, and both wondered how patiently their comrades would be, waiting for them to return. Time could raise doubts in Jib's mind, concerning their safety and whether or not the two may have been captured. Whether their friends waited or became anxious, the result could have consequences, depending on what transpired.

The four dwarfs gathered around the campfire and consumed the fungi along with roasted rabbit ripped apart with disdain. They were a stinky, disgusting lot, lacking any manners or respect for the other, at least when fighting over control of the food. They didn't wash before or after the meal and bounced the stripped bones off an outlying wall.

When they were finished, Alberich wiped his greasy hands on his clothing and made his way to the gold room where the explorers waited to surprise him as he entered. Aiden had pulled his daggers and Hondo his sword when the king stopped at the door, deciding to enter the workshop instead. Hesitant and a little nervous, they followed him in and blocked his escape from the room. The dwarf was so startled; he jumped backward, unable to speak.

"Alberich, I am here for the ring. Tell me where it is and I'll spare your life."

"Who is I?"

"It doesn't matter who I is. Where is the ring?'

Aiden had no intention of taking a life, but without the threat, there was no reason for the king to reveal the location.

The dwarf recovered from his initial shock and exposed a challenging stance and disgusting face, which more than complimented his stench.

"Of what ring do you speak? I have seen no ring nor do I possess one."

"We both know that you do, along with other pilfered treasure. Don't test my patience."

It was an awkward situation for the Egyptian. He could hear the dwarf, but couldn't see him as the two carried on their challenging conversation. Hondo kept his sword pointed toward the source of the invisible voice, but without seeing the position or movements of the dwarf, wondered if his sword really served a purpose.

"How is it you can see me? I should be invisible to your eyes."

"Not to us."

Alberich was confused by the admission and tried touching and adjusting his cloak in an attempt to rectify the invisibility spell, thinking both men could see him and making Hondo feel more comfortable, pointing his blade into nothingness.

"I can still see you, king, no matter what you try. My spell is stronger than yours. Now I'm going to ask you one last time, *where is the ring*?"

"What ring? What ring? I've already told you I know nothing of a ring."

"You are a liar as ignorant as you are ugly. The Rhinegold ring you made from the golden treasure that you stole from the nymphs. You know of what I speak. Hand it over *NOW* so you might live."

"Rhinegold, aah, the maidens are telling lies about me again."

"My magic sees you and through your falsehood as it saw the maidens through their truth. Do you really want to die over something that was never yours to own?"

"If there is a ring, as you say, it could be anywhere. I wouldn't know where to look. It means nothing to me, nothing at all."

The king was stubborn and testing Aiden's threat when the blacksmith noticed a chain around the dwarf's neck. He placed a dagger between the chain and Alberich's throat and, with a quick swipe of the blade, snapped the necklace, sending the ring flying airborne. The dwarf jumped sideways, trying to catch the band, but couldn't match Aiden's reach.

"That's mine. I made it with my own hands. It belongs to me."

"No, it belonged to the maidens, and what was once yours is now mine."

"I will have it back."

"Not today."

"I have the power to take your life."

"You don't possess such powers, but you could take a bath."

With the ring in hand, the two explorers slowly backed out the doorway, keeping their swords pointed at the king and hastily made their retreat for the cave exit.

Alberich screamed out to his fellow dwarfs who drew their small swords and began a swift pursuit. The explorers were faster than the miners and, once they'd reached the mouth of the cave, began stacking loose rocks along the opening. With Jib's help, half the opening was closed off by the time the dwarfs arrived, and a mismatched duel ensued. The disparity was all in the length of the blades, and after suffering a few minor wounds, the dwarfs retreated.

They continued to stack the rocks until the access to the cave was blocked, and they were swiftly on their way again. It would take time for the dwarfs to bind their wounds and clear the rocks, creating a manageable distance, difficult to surmount. If fate was on their side, they would never encounter the king again, but his smell would stay with them for days.

Nymphs, Seers, and Sirens

The following days were spent crossing a snowless pass. Once they reached the optimum altitude, they traveled through the valleys with ease and began their decent to the River Eridanos. If they followed the river to the delta where it entered the Adriatiki Sea, they could sail along the boot to Malta or go upriver to the west coast and catch a boat through the Tyrrhenian Sea to the island of Thrinacia and then on to Malta, according to Jib.

He explained that the inland sea was filled with smaller seas combining to create the larger body as a whole. It was somewhat confusing to the blacksmith, at first, but as long as they could find a vessel to take them to Malta, it really didn't matter.

Approaching the valley below, they could see a major settlement bordering the river. It was the largest concentration of dwellings Aiden had ever seen. Being strangers to the land, they made camp and sent out a hunting party to slay a couple deer. Fresh meat would show they weren't a threat to the people they were about to impose on. Hondo's band returned from the hunt with two bucks. Both were dressed out and the hearts and livers roasted over the fire.

They passed through rows of grapes as the party moved down the final slope. Some of the villagers were picking the crop in a distant section, and on the other side of village were fields of barley, ready to be harvested. The purple fruit had to be tasted by the time they reached the end of the row. The flavor was sweet and juicy with a heavy richness and bouquet, perfect for a great wine.

The one way to enter the settlement was by crossing a bridge spanning a moat. The water was the only defensive element they had, a deterrent at best, but something the blacksmith hadn't seen before. Most homes were built on mounds of black soil. It had to be the darkest soil on earth.

The first structure on the left was a processing site for the grapes. A sizeable wooden press squeezed the juice into a square log vat while workers used ladles to fill large urns and glass containers. The operation was impressive.

Most of the inhabitants had no reaction to the strangers walking through. It was obvious the settlement was accustomed to travelers and traders alike. Jib motioned at two approaching men with a warm and giving gesture to receive the deer on their behalf.

"Thank you, stranger, and welcome to Terramare," one spoke.

"Peace be with you," Jib replied. "Can you tell me where we can find your elders?"

"If you wait, I will show you."

The villager turned, walked a short distance, and found someone else to take his deer. The two talked briefly and he returned.

"You look thirsty. Follow me and the elders will join us."

He led them to a public house next to the open market, with baskets of fruits and vegetables. The pub had tables, chairs, and a wooden bar with a smooth slab top, which was a man's choice.

"What will it be, wine or beer?" the merchant asked.

"It's too early for either. Got any water?" Hondo replied.

"Wine or beer?"

They gave each other a glance and decided, why not. While beer was common in Egypt, they all chose wine, except for Aiden, who decided to try something new. Although the beer was lighter in color, it was much heavier in content. The second round was all about the brew as the Egyptians wanted to compare it to their own. The quality was there even though the taste was different.

Three older men came to join them, and at that point, the meeting was moved to the tables after a short introduction.

"We're grateful for the venison. Please partake with us once it's prepared," Ermete, the more stately of the elders, offered.

He was rather short with sandy gray hair and mustache. His worn and wrinkled face was a result of many seasons in the sun. He projected wisdom in his years and stature among the community.

"It would be our honor," Jib answered.

He explained they were from the Celtic Islands with Egyptian origins, except for the blacksmith, who they were escorting to the coast for transport to their separate destinations. Ermete told them trade ships came up the river every two weeks or so if they wanted to wait for the next call. While they finished their beverage, he encouraged them to tour the various village markets and rejoin him later in the afternoon at the village's grand house in the central hub.

Horse-drawn carts traveled the wide dirt road dissecting the settlement, some carrying ears of corn, others grapes and wheat. They kicked up a light dust from the packed dark soil, leaving shallow ruts behind. The crops owed their quality to the rich earth that blessed this valley.

Agriculture was a vital part of their trade, but so were glassblowing, pottery, and the blacksmith. The forge wasn't used for making weapons, but rather hooks, nails, horseshoes, and other tools. Next to the smithy was a cottage of looms, making rugs as well as weaving rope and a variety of clothing. Their wares hung from metal racks along the road.

Aiden couldn't resist the excellence of the weave, purchasing a blanket and new shirts. The friendly merchants loved to barter and took pride in the merit of their works. Silver was the common currency, but gold held a higher standard and greater purchasing power.

The settlement had a functional layout with crisscrossing side roads, several intersecting at its center. The bank of the river moored several small boats for fishing, but none large enough to sail a sea. Holding pens enclosed sheep, pigs, and chickens. Cows grazed nearby a milking station where two doors down, they made cheese and sold eggs. The village was communal, so everyone benefited from its production and trade.

The visitors were impressed by what they saw and gradually made their way back to the community's hub after a few fine procurements. The grand house had two levels, and all the buildings in the hub had baskets of flowers hanging from their façade and planters layered with bright color.

The elders met them at the front doors to the grand house and ushered them inside. The main room had two stone fireplaces and eight long tables, one crammed with food surrounded by rugs with fish on some and birds on others. The walls were adorned in antlers and two tapestries of local wildlife, both deer and bear, along with several hand-painted murals. Oil lamps hung from the ceiling above the tables for use at night.

The buffet table was filled with fruit, vegetables, venison, pork, fish, and bread, along with options of drink, including milk. It was a fine presentation, and the room began to fill with a throng of residents and other invited travelers. The Egyptians and the blacksmith filled their plates, taking a seat at the first table with Ermete.

"We appreciate your hospitality and are grateful to be received in friendship," Jib announced.

"You provided food for this meal, did you not? We are equally gratified," Ermete replied.

"What will we find farther downriver?"

"Not much till you reach the delta. Seven mature poplars line the riverbank with stones of amber embedded in the soil and riverbed. The trees are the Heliades, seven sisters and daughters of the sun. The gods changed the nymphs into poplars after the death of their brother, and their golden tears turned into brilliant amber stones of light."

"Why were they transformed into trees?" Aiden asked.

"Their beautiful songs became endless cries of sorrow, and it was done to ease their pain of loss. If you stand close enough, you can still hear them cry. Phaethon, their brother, died in the delta. Heavy vapors rise from the marsh where he crashed, and any birds flying over the quagmire plunge to their death in the waters below."

"Crashed?"

"In his father's chariot. The story is folklore, but birds still die and trees continue to shed amber tears."

"Are there any perils other than that of the birds?"

"No, travelers often stop to gather the amber, although we try to keep it secret. We harvest the stones ourselves for making rings, bracelets, and necklaces. The jewelry and stones are highly desirable on the trade market."

"If we could borrow a boat, I'd like to see it for myself."

"Our fishermen would gladly take you there. We could use more of the gems ourselves."

"Tomorrow then?"

"I will arrange it."

After finishing the meal, the travelers went to the village inn across the road and paid for a night's stay. The rooms were small, but adequate, with fresh cut flowers and a feather bed. It was the most comfortable night's sleep the blacksmith could remember. In the morning, he felt so relaxed and refreshed, he hesitated leaving the softness of the mattress.

They departed the inn and headed toward the waters' edge to bathe and meet the fishermen taking them downriver. Until they arrived at the docks, the talk was all about their undisturbed night's sleep and how rested and renewed they felt. Rejuvenated by the cool water and fresh clean shirts, they were ready to sail the small boats to the delta.

Two vessels awaited them with one fisherman each to pilot the voyage to the mouth feeding the sea. The journey would take a day's travel each way with nothing much to do but enjoy the warmth of the sun. It was their first real break since leaving the island, and they took advantage of every moment.

It was almost sunset before the poplar grove came into view. The grand trees were nature's bond with the rich black earth, their branches reaching out like they were holding hands and consoling each other. The marshes' exhaled vapor was also present, but no birds were anywhere near the misty cloud.

The sails were lowered, and the boats were grounded as the sun descended behind the mountains, its fading light casting a golden hue on the stones resting at their feet. There were thousands of smooth translucent ingots of gold scattered up and down the beach. Aiden wondered why so many tears were surrendered in easing the Heliades' loss and how many years were enough to satisfy their gods. Was Phaethon's mortality measured through the immortality of his sisters' undying grief and would the trees shed tears eternally? How could so much beauty reflect such sadness? It was difficult to understand such a quandary.

The blacksmith gathered a handful of gems, stuffing them in his right front pocket on his way to set camp near the poplars. Hondo started a fire with wood the fishermen had loaded in the boats, and everyone settled in for the night. Stories were shared around the circle with the hot topic centered on the quest itself. The fishermen were fascinated, having no adventures beyond their own valley, but still plenty to impart.

Aiden's sleep was interrupted by the sounds of sorrowful cries. The eerie songs of sadness were disturbing, and soon, everyone was awake. The blacksmith couldn't resist the call from the trees and had to listen in their presence. He was astounded to see how their roots resembled feet and a faint facial outline was noticeable in the bark. Sap oozed out of the trunk and branches, dripping to the ground. He could deeply feel the influence of their pain, shedding his own tears in remorse.

The power of the sisters was dominating his emotion and the others as well. It was difficult to walk away from their distressing control and agonizing heartbreak, but somehow, he found the willpower to overcome their unbearable cries.

He managed to pull away from the Heliades' reign over emotion by plunging his ears and finally felt some relief. He'd never felt such an overwhelming lack of control over his own feelings. As he stood at a distance from the grove, Aiden noticed a horned owl perched in one of the poplars and became suspicious. He felt like he was being watched and wondered what magic was in play. Had the owl played an impact on his experience, or was it just his imagination?

The blacksmith maintained his focus on the bird, returning its stare for a short time before the owl took flight. He could see a faint outline of a woman as he followed its path across the vapors of the marsh, with no effect on the bird, and knew his instinct was right. Whether it was a spell or a shape-shifter, someone was monitoring their movements, and they would have to heed any unusual events in the future. For now, they had to show caution, not knowing the purpose behind such powers.

Once the sun came up, they could no longer hear the cries or feel the enchantment of the Heliades. They collected the needed amber gems and sailed back up the river, taking turns catching up on lost sleep. Sailing against the current slowed the return to the settlement; they arrived after dark. The boats were tied up, and they headed to the inn to satisfy their thirst. Beer was the beverage of choice as they sat around a wooden table to weigh their options of travel.

"Right now, we're about halfway between the Adriatiki and Tyrrhenian Seas. We've been to the delta, and there may not be a ship here for two more weeks. We might be able to find a ride to the islands faster if we head west. What do you think is best?" Jib asked.

"You're right, we've been to the delta and heard the sisters cry. It was a painful experience I'd rather not repeat. I'm for heading west," Aiden replied.

Everyone nodded in agreement and their course was set. The vote left them discussing the Heliades until the intoxication overcame their speech and they held each other up as they sought out their beds.

When morning came, they, nursing mild hangovers, met at the public house for scrambled eggs and ham. Ermete was doing the same, and they shared their decision with the elder. He offered to have a fishing boat take them upriver; it was his way of thanking them for the amber stones. They accepted his offer and shopped the food markets before heading back to the docks for their ferry west.

The fisherman sailed as far upriver as the craft would take them. Well after sunset, he stayed the night before heading back. The remainder of the westward journey was across the northern plains and took three days to reach the coast. They built a large bonfire on the beach and waited another two days before spotting the first vessel.

It was a large two-masted penteconter with a crow's nest that didn't appear to be a merchant ship. Its dark sides looked ominous, and they considered the possibility of pirates. The ship, seeing their fire as it drew closer, yielded the sails and manned the fifty oars. It dropped anchor in the shallows and lowered a launch with four sailors rowing to shore. If they were pirates, the odds were on the side of the Egyptians who awaited the landing with one hand on their swords.

Fears soon subsided when they realized one of the sailors was a woman, a rare sight and bad luck to most crews. They pulled the launch onto the beach and stood, each group checking out the other with the blacksmith making the first move.

"My name's Aiden, and we're looking for transport to Thrinacia or Malta, if you are headed that way and can oblige us."

"I'm Jason, captain of the Argo. We sail to the Phaeacian Islands. We can accommodate you there, but what are you doing in this remote place?"

"It's a long story and a distant journey, but I'm on a quest."

"My story too is a long one. I've also been on a quest except I've completed mine."

"Then we have something in common."

"We do. Where are you from?"

"The Celtic Islands. I'm a blacksmith."

"Atalanta is a Spartan blacksmith. That makes two things in common," Jason said as he motioned toward his female companion.

Aiden met her glance, one of acceptance, and found her much too beautiful to be a blacksmith. She had long reddish-brown hair, luscious curves, yet the build of a warrior. She carried a bow and a leather sheath with a wrap that barely met her knees.

"I'm Jib, an Egyptian and Aiden's escort to Malta. I mean no disrespect, but isn't it unlucky to have a woman aboard ship?"

"It is. I told her she couldn't go on this voyage, but she's no ordinary woman."

"No's not in my vocabulary. I'm more than equal to any man here," she responded.

"And she's proven that more times than I can count. We have room on board if you're willing to share your fire."

"Indeed," Jib agreed to the invitation.

The huskiest of the four, clad in a lion skin, waved to the moored ship, and soon another launch approached the beach while Jason's long boat returned to receive another load. The captain and Aiden shook hands and took a seat on a log near the fire soon joined by Atalanta.

"So what's the purpose of your quest?" Jason asked.

He wore a Pilos helmet over his long dark blond hair, a deep-brown wrap with a red sash, and sandals that stretched to his knees. He was medium build with firm muscles, but not overly so.

"I'm on a quest for a phoenix feather and the hand of a princess."

"Classic, a quest always seems to have royal roots of some type, does it not?"

"Evidently and your quest?"

"Mine was for the fleece of a golden winged ram, guarded by a dragon that never slept. With Medea's sleeping potion, it was easy to acquire. I needed the hide to claim my rightful seat on the throne of Lolcus in Thessaly. It's stowed in my cabin aboard the Argo. You know, Atalanta is a princess of Arcadia. You might win her heart without a feather."

"You're not like any princess I've ever seen."

"Nor likely to ever see again. Think of me, more, as a man in a woman's body. There's nothing refined or dainty about me."

"You look all woman to me, a fine match for a warrior."

"That's one reason to explain my passage. There is one I find suitable, but he's already spoken for."

"She's talking about me and Medea, a princess and priestess in her own right. She helped me acquire the fleece with her magic potion, and we plan to marry when we return to Greece."

"True, but I'm a much finer match than she, except for her sorcery. My enhancement is strictly physical in nature. She can't compete with that."

"Who's the husky, muscular man in the lion skin?"

"That's Periclymenus, the shape-shifting son of Poseidon, he's pretending to be Heracles, a Greek hero. His physical strength is that of many men and his courage unmatched. Heracles' accomplishments are legendary because he has no fear. He doesn't need a weapon to be deadly, with his powerful muscles, he can easily crush a man. Unfortunately, he got left behind at Cios."

When Medea came ashore to join Jason, Atalanta reluctantly moved to another log with new conversation and more introductions. The priestess was formidable, her physical attributes capable of enticing any man. She had long brown hair and wore a long burgundy gown, which emphasized her full, plump breasts and the curve of her hips. She had the appearance of a princess, but overdressed for a voyage. She gracefully sat and wrapped her arm around the captain.

"Medea, my love, this is Aiden. He's a Celt on a quest for the feather of the phoenix."

"He'll need some magical help with that."

"I have my resources, priestess or princess, do you have a preference?"

"Priestess, potions and enchantments are my craft. Do you possess any skill in the dark arts?"

"None, I have to rely on a wizard for that and my own common sense."

"Does the wizard travel with you?"
"No, he stayed behind."
"He must be powerful to be effective from such a distance. Is he your only resource?"
"Not exactly, I do have Alberich's golden ring, made from the treasure stolen from the Rhinegold Maidens, and a ruby necklace, said to attract the phoenix."
"You do travel in dark circles. The ring of the Nibelungen king has power if you know how to use it and you survived the dwarf, the nymphs, and the siren, or you wouldn't be here. Impressive, you'd make a fine Argonaut, but there are other dark forces in play. You have no idea who you're messing with."
"You mean Lilith?"
"I'm surprised you know of her. She's the most powerful witch, you'd never want to meet, the queen of the dark arts and goddess of hell. She is my high priestess, and she'll use all her powers to reclaim the ring. I wouldn't want to be in your shoes, and there is nothing I can do to help you."
"So I've been told."
"Good luck, but you'll need far more than luck. I'm sure her eyes are upon your every move."
"In the form of a horned owl, I'm sure."
"Then you've seen each other, but she can change her form at will and that's all I can say."
"Jason, it must be challenging with two women onboard?"
"You have no idea. Neither one would accept my rejection. I was forced to make a pact that allowed Medea to sail with me in order to capture the fleece. I'm not sure I'd have been able to do it without her help. It is somewhat uncomfortable for the men, and the women can be contentious, but we've learned to tolerate their presence."
"We keep them in line, besides, I'll soon be his wife, the queen, and he'll have to give this all up."

With kegs of wine and beer on the beach, male egos began to dominate the evening. It took more than a dozen Argonauts to wrestle the mock Heracles to the sand with a little help from the herbs Medea had slipped in his drink. Atalanta took advantage of the male esteem to best each in turn, proving her worth, not only in stature, but her ability to out drink most men. Aiden was astounded by the behavior of a crew, with royal blood flowing through its veins, even though they were wildly entertaining.

The aggressive conduct of the Argonauts settled down once Orpheus, the musician and father of song, began to play his golden lyre said to charm animals of every sort, and the music seemed to be working its magic. Aiden wasn't sure if it was the drink or the music, but soon, they all sprawled out on the sandy beach.

Thetis sounded the ship's horn, stirring the sleeping crew as the sound pierced through the thin morning fog. Hangovers were aplenty as they staggered to their feet and prepared to reboard the ship. Aiden was eager to embark the Argo and get his quest back underway, and the Egyptians were only days from finding a vessel to take them home. Once all were on deck, they pulled anchor and manned the fifty oars, taking the boat to deeper water.

With sails raised and Theseus in the crow's nest, the Argo continued its voyage south along the coast. Euphemus, the ship's helmsman, guided the swift vessel through the reasonably calm water and mild wind as Aiden and Jason joined him at the wheel.

"Jason, you will wander endlessly across the sea if you do not sail to Aeaea. Circe must cleanse Medea for the death of her brother Apsyrtus," the prow spoke.

"You have a talking boat?" Aiden asked, stunned by the voice.

"We do. The prow was cut from the talking tree of the sacred forest of Dodona. It guides and protects us through prophecy," Jason said proudly.

"Unbelievable. How reliable are the prophecies?"

"Very accurate, we wouldn't be here if we didn't heed the warnings."

"Where is Aeaea?"

"Not far, it's called the Isle of the Dawn. Medea's aunt Circe has a palace there."

"Isle of the Dawn?"

"Circe is a goddess of magic, or witch, depending on who you talk to. She can block out sun or moon with clouds, enough to hide her island."

"Have you been there before?"

"Never."

"What happened to Medea's brother?"

"He was the captain of the Colchian fleet pursuing us for the fleece and Medea, thinking she was kidnapped. When it appeared they had our access to the Danube delta blocked, we convinced Apsyrtus he could have Medea if he allowed the Argo to pass. He agreed and I killed him while we were making the trade so the Colchians wouldn't follow us."

Jason left to find Medea and share the words from the prow. He wondered what her relationship with her aunt was like and how she felt about being cleansed. Soon the two arrived at the helm where Medea asked the prow to repeat the prophecy, which it did. Medea didn't seem bothered by the threat, easing any doubt in Jason's mind.

It was late afternoon when the prow sliced through the deep blue water surrounding the island. Jason and Medea stood on the bow, fanning the horizon with a spyglass, when the prow announced their arrival.

The island came into view with a heavy mist enveloping the canopy yet leaving the beach clear and visible. Several maidens in gleaming dresses hovered like dragonflies over the sand, joined by a number of wild wolves, lions, and bears beneath them. The Argo lowered the sails again and rowed the ship to shallower water, dropping the anchor.

As Jason, Medea, Aiden, and two more Argonauts navigated the launch toward the beach, the maidens landed on the shore among the animals, their see-through, silky, lustrous gowns dragging the sand. Medea jumped into the coastal surf, cautioning the others to wait in the boat and waded ashore. The maidens waved their hands and called the men to the island.

"Refrain to land here, Argonauts. On this island, men have become beasts, a consequence of Circe's potions," Medea cried out in a hearty voice.

Once her words were spoken, the maidens shrunk away until they were nothing, and the wildness of the beasts became tame. The animals began to whine, peering on the priestess with their human eyes. She stroked their fur and called her party to shore where they, too, petted the creatures.

"Take me to Circe's temple without delay," she demanded.

Jason and Medea went on alone while the rest sat on the launch and waited. The two followed the animals into the hazy tree line and disappeared. When they returned to the beach an hour later, Circe came with them, along with her maidens who carried gold baskets filled with stemmed flowers. She wore a long purple robe and a golden veil, covering the tresses of her flaming-red hair.

The three went to the waters' edge where the witch washed her niece's body, then her clothes with seawater. Once the purification was absolute, Medea was given a cup of fresh water to drink, and all three walked toward the launch, with Circe giving the priestess one last vision.

"You will ask a woman of wisdom what you are to do with your life. Heed her advice."

Aiden stood there as they approached, with his oar pointing skyward. A redheaded woodpecker suddenly appeared, attacking the oar with its beak.

"Pay him no mind, it's just Picus trying to get your attention. He was a young magician who spurned my love and advances. He won't be able to do that anymore, will he?" Circe advised sarcastically as she turned without any further greetings and walked back up the beach to her temple.

Her maidens tossed all the flowers into the surf and then flew away, with the silk hugging their naked bodies as it blew in the wind. With Medea cleansed and forgiven for her brother's assassination, they returned to the Argo and set sail once again.

"Could you do anything to give those men back their manhood?" Aiden asked the priestess as they stood on the bow and watched the island fade away.

"I already did, but they won't realize it until they drink the water from the trough. I prepared a potion before we landed for that very purpose. I hope they escape before my aunt discovers what I've done. She won't be pleased with me."

"I'm finding out more every day, what a strange world I live in, among such bizarre characters. What a story I can tell, even if the wizard is the only one to believe me."

"Any good wizard will already know, but welcome to my world, where the normal is strange."

The Argo crashed the waves as they sailed farther south in the Tyrrhenian Sea. The blacksmith felt refreshed as the mist splashed his face and the wind blew his hair. As the sky drew darker, he realized he had no choice but to sleep on deck, and his stomach was already starting to churn. He'd never slept aboard a vessel as it bounced across the waves. The thought alone was enough to leave him hanging over the side of the ship, but he wasn't alone, Dak and Hondo were on either side. It would be a long, nauseous, and sleepless night.

By morning, the stomach cramps had taken their toll, and all three felt very weak. Medea approached the sickened travelers with a hint of a smile.

"I have a potion for that."

"Where were you last night?" Aiden asked.

"In the captain's cabin, but we could still hear your misery. I couldn't mix the herbs until morning, but if you drink from the glass now, it will remedy your seasickness for the rest of your life."

"That's a relief. I'd get dangerously thin and weak if I continued to purge day after day. Thanks."

The three men drank the potion and the results were immediate. They each found a dark corner below deck to catch some winks until late in the morning when they reappeared with color in their faces. Now when Aiden hung over the side, he followed the dolphins, whose swimming speed matched that of the Argo. It was another two uneventful days of sailing before the prow spoke another prophecy.

"We near Anthemoessa, island of the siren Aphrodite. The Argo will not pass the enchantment of her song without the help of Orpheus."

Atalanta went to Jason's cabin to summon the musician away from his conversation with the captain and the priestess. The two women exchanged taunting looks before she spoke.

"The prow has spoken. We near the isle of the sirens and only Orpheus can protect us, I mean, the men, since the sirens have no effect on Medea and me. Our vulnerability is only with each other," she said with a forced smile and left.

"Can't we drop her off somewhere along this voyage?" the priestess asked, hoping for confirmation from the captain.

"If you find her so annoying, why not concoct a potion to mellow her behavior and satisfy your displeasure?"

"I can do that, but she'd still be onboard and I'd still have to look at her."

When they reached the helm, Orpheus had already begun to play his golden lyre, drowning out the songs of enchantment. His music was more beautiful than theirs, rescinding their power and appeal over the crew. It wasn't long before two sirens, with bird wings and exposed feminine features, fluttered between the masts, annoyed that their voices had no impact on the men, and the musician only played louder.

Unable to match the quality of the lyre, they flew closer to their victims, but Orpheus followed each move they made. The crew compounded their anger when they began to sing as loud as they could. The sirens hovered, trying to grab any man they could to carry them away, and when that didn't work, they attempted to knock the lyre out of the musician's hands.

Dak seized a long-handled gaff, jousting it skyward, only to have Aphrodite rip it out of his hands. She flipped it around and used the hook to snare his shirt, lifting his feet off the deck. He gripped the handle and tried to release himself, but it wasn't until members of the crew wrapped their arms around his legs, pulling him back, that his shirt ripped and he fell backward on the planks. The siren attempted to snag the Egyptian several times as he rolled around beneath her. The assault continued several minutes until finally, the sirens gave up and flew away.

"Persistent, aren't they?" Aiden said.

"That's why they are who they are. Both were handmaidens to the goddess Persephone when she was kidnapped by Haides while picking fresh flowers in the meadow. Her mother, Demeter, gave them wings of birds to help search for her daughter. They settled on this island after Demeter made a pact with Haides to release the goddess, but only for half the seasons. Since Persephone was the goddess of the spring bounty, she had to return to the underworld in the winter months, thus making her goddess of two different worlds during opposite times of the year," Medea explained.

"How do you know all that?"

"Because Orpheus's true love is the lovely Persephone. The story is part of my culture and knowledge of the dark arts. I'm a priestess devoted to the goddess Hecater who has been involved at a high level in such things."

"Orpheus will visit her in the underworld," the prow interrupted the conversation.

"Who, Hecater?" the musician asked.

"Persephone."

"Why would Persephone, my true love, be in the underworld? Death is the only entry to the dark world of Hades. Has she died?" the musician asked.

"Today she lives."

"And tomorrow?"

"It's not for me to answer."

Orpheus was overcome by the revelation. He was still far from home, powerless to intercede on his wife's behalf and unable to gain any other information, even through Medea.

Spirits of the Sea

With another challenge overcome and behind them, the Argonauts sailed on for the island off the coast of Greece where everyone would go their own way. It was another beautiful, cloudless day with a slight southerly wind and birds following their progress along the coast.

Meanwhile, Edric was summoned to the castle in order to provide King Darian with an update. He was relieved the king hadn't chosen to visit him instead, which had only happened once some time ago, when the queen was sick. The wizard's vision was grave, indeed, and he never returned again at least so far.

When Edric neared the vestibule, the door was open and the princess was with the king. He wasn't surprised and waited to be welcomed. With a wave of a hand, the wizard entered and joined them at the grand table. The princess filled their three empty glasses with wine, and Edric prepared to answer the king's questions the best that he could.

"You know why you're here?"

"I do."

"It's been three weeks. What of the quest?"

"Sire, one more has drowned, six have returned, and seventeen remain on the quest. The other seven have died by various means."

"I see, a large number have already failed. Did I make this challenge too difficult to succeed?"

"Sire, it's not for me to say, but the best of the best have survived thus far."

The wizard could see the king was disturbed with the shrinking number. Ariana, on the other hand, was beaming since the best meant Aiden was still in pursuit of the feather. The two opposite facial expressions seemed strange, occurring at the same time. The king had no further questions, but the princess wouldn't be so easy. She escorted Edric down the hall to the compound where it was her turn to grill the wizard.

"It was a relief to find Aiden is still alive. Can you tell me where he is?"

The wizard was cautious about giving too much information. Ariana had never viewed the cauldron or the mirror, and Edric had to preserve their secrecy.

"All I can tell you is that I sense Aiden is aboard a large ship on the inland sea."

"Does he still have the Egyptian escort, or is he alone?"

"He is not alone."

"And is he well?"

"He is and in good spirit."

The princess was satisfied, but still had a look on her face that begged to ask more questions. She thanked him, and the two went their separate ways with Edric returning to his mirror for a view of the Argo's progress.

Aboard the Argo, Medea made her way to the helm where Jason, Aiden, and Orpheus stood near the helmsman.

"We are nearing the Symphlegades very soon and must make preparations."

"Symphlegades?" Jason asked.

"It's a passage between Thrinacia and the mainland with two immense crashing rocks and the evil spirits of Scylla and Charibdis. They will do everything in their power to destroy the Argo and its crew."

"How will they do that?"

"Many ways. First, you'll face the crashing waves and whirlpools of Charibdis, trying to swamp the boat and suck it down in the depths. If you make it past that, wandering rocks will try to take out your hull. In between, the crashing rocks will come together and smash what's left, leaving Scylla to devour your crew on the other side."

"My god, has any ship ever made it through such a passage, and who would ever want to try?"

"Odysseus did, losing six of his crew, but they sailed a much smaller vessel."

"What do we need to do?"

"Tie everything down that you can. Most of the crew should be held below deck, or they will be swept overboard and don't man the crow's nest. Bring oars from below so some of the crew can use them to push us away from the moving rocks, and before we attempt to pass between the sea spirits, we need to bring a dove from below and release it to measure the time it takes for the rocks to crash together."

"We'll do that. Anything else?"

"Thetis should be manning the helm, his abilities will improve our chances, other than that, we wait for the prow to announce our arrival."

At the gatehouse, the wizard's view through the mirror was interrupted by a bang at his door. The peephole revealed the princess, standing on the other side.

"I know you're in there, Edric, answer the door. I won't go away until you do."

The princess had never knocked before this, catching the wizard off guard, but he knew she was destined to find his door sooner rather than later, and ignoring her knock would not make her go away. She began pounding again.

"Edric, answer the door. Don't make me get my father."

One caller was enough; two would only serve to compound the issue. He delayed opening the door, but there was no other option.

"Mister Wizard, it will be easier for both of us if we don't involve my father. I have but one interest, and he could have many."

He knew she was right. The quest was her only interest while the king could have renewed questions about the future of his kingdom that might never stop. The princess banged again, and he finally opened to greet her.

"Ariana, it's good to see you again."

"Let's not kid ourselves. Edric, you and I both know you didn't want to open this door. I'm coming in, with or without your invitation, but I'd rather you welcome me."

"Your Highness," the wizard said reluctantly as he motioned her in.

She didn't seem surprised by the contents on the walls or grand table and walked directly to the hearth and took a seat. This was a conversation the wizard had hoped to avoid, but it was inevitable.

"Can I get you something to drink?"

"Water would be fine, thank you."

Ariana scanned the walls in more detail while the wizard poured the water. The mirror was the only thing to pique her interest as she accepted her refreshment.

"You know more than you're telling, Edric, and now is the time to reveal your secrets to me. My father doesn't have to know I've been here unless you choose."

"What do you want to know?"

"Everything you do. This about my life and my future, is it not?"

"Indeed."

"Then it's my right to know."

"If you think you're ready."

"I'm not the helpless princess that people think I am, and there's nothing you could tell me that would be that shocking."

"I'm not so sure. This quest is more complicated than you think."

The wizard started with the channel crossing without disclosing the source of his information. He noticed her facial expressions change more and more as the story of expedition moved forward. At times, she just shook her head, and at others, it was the fear written on her face, even a tear, until the journey was up-to-date.

"How do you know this to be true? What magic brings your vision?"

"My visions are revealed through my dreams."

"Wizard, there are more than dreams at play here. What is the purpose of the mirror?"

"It's just a mirror."

"A mirror to what? I'd like to know."

"Just a mirror."

"I think there's more, how does it work?"

The wizard stood at the mirror, pretending it was as he said, but the princess proved hard to please as she examined it closely.

"Your visions have more detail than one would receive through dreams, so tell me, how does it work?"

Edric realized the princess was somehow more in tune than he gave her credit. Maybe it was her love for Aiden, or possibly, she had an undeveloped sense in the arts. Either way, he had no choice but to open the portal. He passed his hand before the glass without any shocking reaction from Ariana.

"I knew there was more to this than just dreams. Why have you kept this from me?"

"My lady, I keep this from everyone. A wizard should never have to divulge the sources of his visionary powers. I share only what people can handle or what's most necessary to disclose. Nothing more, nothing less."

The princess was pleased to see her love and touched the mirror with her hand, causing the vision to disappear.

"Bring him back."

"I will, but don't touch the mirror again. The effect will interrupt the revelation."

"Where is he now?"

"Approaching the most dangerous challenge faced thus far, the Symphlegades."

He explained the hazards of the passage in detail, which she handled quite well, except for a few more tears rolling down her face.

"Will they pass safely?"

"I can't tell you, they're too far away for me to view future events."

"How long before they reach the rocks?"
"Two, maybe three hours."

"I want to be here when they do. Is that clear?"
"Yes, my lady."
"I will return and share our secrets with no one."

She turned and gracefully walked out the door, leaving the wizard to expect her. There was no way to protect her from the truth if she wanted to see for herself. The outcome facing the Argo could be disastrous, right before her very eyes.

With Thetis at the helm, the nervous crew awaited word from the prow. Only a dozen men held oars above deck, including Aiden and Jib. The captain stood at the bow with his eyeglass while Medea remained in his cabin with Orpheus and the dove. Then finally word came.

"Beware, Charibdis approaches."

Jason could see whirlpools encroaching on both sides of the Argo; using his arms, he signaled Thetis the changing navigational directions until the prow took over the task.

Ariana had returned to the gatehouse, just in time to see the Argo enter the crashing waves with Aiden manning an oar. The wizard told her to view but ask no questions since he couldn't change the outcome of the passage, so she did what she was asked.

"Port!" the prow screeched as Thetis made his first swift adjustment.

The sudden turn knocked half the crew off their feet, and they scrambled to regain their footing as the crashing waves washed across the wooden deck.

"Starboard."

With almost the same result, except now the ship's pitch from bow to stern was equally excessive to the sway from port to starboard. Jason, still standing above the prow, was drenched with every wave. He stood steadfast, determined the sea would not control his destiny.

The ship's wheel was turning faster than the prow could speak, leaving Thetis to react on impulse as the guidance went silent. The Argo slipped past the first whirlpool, but was caught in the second, spinning the ship in a clockwise rotation until the helmsman was able to pull the ship out and into a third eddy, spinning the boat in the opposite direction. The crew grabbed anything they could to prevent themselves from being washed overboard as the ship's pitch left them staring into the eye of the whirlpool, losing three of the oars in the process.

Their situation looked hopeless as the Argo made its fourth rotation, sinking deeper into the mouth of Charibdis with every spin. Suddenly, a gust of wind caught the sails with enough force to right the ship and alter their course. Waves continued to bash the sides of the vessel, but the deadly whirlpools were behind them and the wandering rocks lay dead ahead.

"That was scary," Ariana said with a sigh of relief, her hands still touching her cheeks as she viewed through the portal.

"That was only the beginning. It gets worse," the wizard warned. "Are you sure you're up for this?"

"I wouldn't want to be anywhere else."

Everyone prepared themselves for the next test as the prow announced the arrival of the moving rocks. With oars in hand, the crew began pushing the ship away from the gradually stirring rocks as they adjusted to the Argo course from either side. The rocks had minds of their own, guided by the sea spirit and were determined to destroy the hull.

Three oars snapped as the rocks made contact on both sides of the ship, simultaneously knocking every man down, including Jason, but leaving the integrity of the hull intact. They were back on their feet as quickly as they went down, each man drenched to their souls. The number of rocks was countless, and the crew's stamina and determination was all that separated them from disaster.

Another rock hit the starboard side with less force, but the men still lost their footing. So far, the Argo had managed to avoid striking any at the head where the ship was most vulnerable, and any collision at the bow would certainly compromise the hull, concluding in their demise.

Thetis was reaching a point of exhaustion at the helm, fighting the wheel in a test of endurance. Twice the wheel spun out of control as he fought to regain a solid grip, feeling the pain in every muscle of his body. Jason could see his anguish, but there was no other man capable of withstanding the extraordinary demands of the helm.

Another gust of wind filled the sails as the vessel grazed two more rocks. The gusts had been timely so far, but Jason knew they could turn deadly just as fast. There were only a half a dozen rocks separating the Argo from the passage as the wind died down once more. The crew was knocked to the deck one last time before it was over and behind them.

Remarkably, the ship was still in one piece and, for the moment, floating in reasonably calm water. With the sheer walls of the passage drawing near, Jason retrieved the dove from his cabin with Medea and Aiden following him to the bow.

"If the dove makes it through the passage, Jason, then we should too," Medea advised.

"And what if it doesn't?"

"Then we have to take our chances. Going forward is our only option unless you want to revisit the moving rocks and whirlpools."

"No, we were lucky to pass the first time."

Jason released the dove as the waves began to rise and crash into one another again. The bird flew as straight as an arrow, flapping its wings wildly as if it knew speed was its ally. Everyone's focus was on the dove as it entered the pass, and the vertical walls began to move slowly toward each other, sensing the space between was being invaded.

Timing was going to be everything. Not only did the dove have to clear the closing passage safely, the walls had to open up again before the Argo entered or it would be crushed. There was uneasiness among the crew as they continued to watch the flapping wings and the encroaching walls, then the three came together. They were devastated until the two sides began to open, exposing the dove minus one tail feather floating gently in the air. The dove had cleared safely.

It was the Argo's turn next, but the ship was no bird. It was a tense moment when all the crew came topside. Their experience with the first two challenges was felt, but unseen, although they were just as wet and battered. The ship was closing fast on the passage while the gap continued to widen.

Tremendous waves were generated by the movement of the walls, which reached their expanse at the same time the ship penetrated the gap. The momentary lapse of the walls changing direction would give the Argo a few more precious seconds to clear the hazard. All they needed now was another gust of wind to catch the sails.

The walls started to close with a grinding sound, not heard during the dove's flight, as if they were working harder than before to crush their prey. It was an eerie feeling, watching the stone barriers converge on the ship, pushing ever closer by the moment. Where was the wind when they really needed that extra push through the gap?

The ship was only a third of the way through the channel when the wind died, completely. Had sinister forces, in their anger and frustration, brought about the disturbing calm? The Argo was helpless without a breeze to cut through the turbulent water. Jason sent the crew below to break out the oars. He wasn't sure whether or not it would help increase the ship's speed, but it was worth a try.

Medea sensed the serious nature of the situation. The wind had saved them twice, and without its help, the Argo and its crew would be obliterated. She went to the captain's quarters, sat at the table, and lit a candle. She made a desperate and spiritual plea to the gods of the wind for help. First, she appealed to Notus, the god of the south wind, and then prayed to Lips of the southeast wind.

She continued to petition their help as the boat rocked to and fro with increasing force. The candleholder slid across the table and into her hands. She resumed her dyer prayers, asking them to acknowledge her summons by blowing out the flame of the candle. The priestess was relentless, and soon her requests became demands as she continued to repeat her passionate urging for help.

Below deck, the Argonauts struggled to use the oars effectively as the violent waves crashed against both sides of the ship. Half the time they were rowing air and the other half, the oars were submerged in water. Their efforts were making little difference, but they wouldn't give up the fight, even though two more oars splintered under the intense force of the waves. They were rowing more independently than together with oars smacking each other.

Jason could see their futile efforts were doing almost nothing to increase their speed. They were only halfway, the walls were closing in, and soon they'd be too close to use the oars anyway, so he cancelled his order and had his men return topside with the oars. Below deck, they'd be crushed, but above, the oars could be used as poles against the rock to help push them along.

They were fifty yards from sanity before they could ply the oars. The idea was working, but Jason could see it wouldn't be enough to save them, utter destruction was inevitable. The crew stepped back and waited for the collision.

With a sudden whiff of air, Medea's candle was extinguished, and she knew she'd been heard. The gods were listening to her plea, and she thanked them. When she stepped out of the cabin, she could feel the wind in her hair and see the gust catch the sails. It was a beautiful and blessed sight to behold.

Jason stood at the bow with the breeze at his back and felt the Argo swiftly lurch forward. The bow was clear, yet only inches separated the ship from the rocks. The wind hadn't let him down, and there was still a good chance they could survive the divisive curse of the sea spirits.

The captain hurriedly moved aft against the stiffening wind, keeping his eyes on both encroaching walls. Once astern, he was met by a majority of the crew, just as the rock touched the starboard side first, pushing the ship into the opposite wall, scrapping off paint in the process.

The Argo was being squeezed, and the wood began to creak under the pressure. Wind was working against the stone as waves hammered the hull, lifting the tail up slightly.

They were only inches away from the sea if the ship could escape the vise that compressed them. Unexpectedly, nails popped out of a crossing beam above the rudder releasing the Argo and leaving the beam stuck between the rocks. The ship was free; they had cheated death and the damage astern was minor. The wind had redefined their fate.

A celebration ensued. For a moment, the crew was out of control, though the merriment was well deserved. The Argo hadn't lost a man unlike Odysseus. The priestess shared her appeal to the gods of the wind with Jason and the Argonauts. They knew they were both fortunate and lucky that the gods paid them any mind at all, and they were grateful.

"I don't know how they deal with all that stress. I can barely handle it myself and I'm viewing the events from a distance," the princess admitted to the wizard.

"Aiden expected challenges and danger were imminent, but nothing like what he's been through so far, and they still have to face a second encounter with the moving rocks and then, Scylla, the serpent. It isn't over yet, and it's likely the challenges will continue throughout his travels."

"It's all so frustrating."

"Now you know why I hesitated to share any details of expedition with you."

She just nodded, holding her chalice of wine with both hands, then took another large swig to calm her nerves.

Jason interrupted the crew's rejoicing, reminding them the moving rocks and whirlpools on the southern side were growing very near. It took a few seconds of thought before the realization was absorbed, and the men were scrambling to prepare.

"Shifting rocks ahead," the prow announced.

Jason, with his eyeglass, counted a much smaller number of slumbering stone islands on this side of the passage. The lesser stood silent near the starboard shore, and the captain set his course. The closest rocks started moving, once ship had declared, but this time, they passed the obstacles unscathed.

Going with the current, the rushing waters flushed through the widening channel, increasing the Argo's speed and making the crossing of whirlpools much easier too. The ship still had a wild ride, spinning a couple times, but they avoided laying the boat on its side. The crew felt confident as they reached the open sea with Thrinacia on one side and the boot on the other, but somewhere in the open waters, Scylla, the sea dragon, lay in wait.

Jason handed Aiden his eyeglass and gave the blacksmith a chance to view the water from the crow's nest. He was more than willing since the potion had eliminated his sickness, and he wouldn't be hanging his head over the side of the basket. The channel continued to widen and separate the two shores with nothing creating an unusual wake.

The captain stood on the bow, scanning both sides of the ship. The serpent was no small creature, which should make it easy to spot, but the sea was void of anything threatening. The priestess joined him at the bow.

"See anything?" she asked.

"No, do serpents sleep?"

"Not likely, with the ship in open water. She knows we're here."

"What's she waiting for?"

"Scylla holds the element of surprise. Maybe she's waiting for you to make a critical mistake."

"I don't make mistakes."

"Jason, you forget I know you too well, besides, the only purpose in allowing you to see her from a distance would be to cause panic among the crew."

"Scylla draws near," the prow advised.

"Where? I don't see anything."

"What makes you think she wants you to?"

"Aiden, stay alert, she's out there and very close."

The entire crew kept an open eye on the water, including along the Argo's sides, but still nothing. Emotions swayed between impatience and fear as the crew waited and waited for something to happen.

Suddenly, with no warning, something hit the hull with such force, the ship lifted out of the water and crashed back down. The serpent had arrived, but was still unseen. Her attack was brief as she tested the Argo's vulnerability, and then, an eerie calm and a creepy silence followed. They waited for her to strike the hull again as time seemed to last an eternity.

Jib picked up one of the splintered oar handles off the deck and realized it was sharp enough to use as a spear. Hondo followed his lead, grabbing one for himself, and the two moved to opposite flanks. Both were exceptional with a lance if she would only show herself.

The serpent struck from another direction, elevating the boat once more while damaging the rudder in the process. Aiden found himself swaying with the mast as he viewed a long shadow, no one else could see, moving beneath the surface. The image was very large, moving fast and deep enough to reveal no detail.

"Jason, she's damaged the rudder," Thetis voiced in frustration.

"She's smart, very smart. With a strong wind and no steering, she could scuttle us on either rocky beach."

"The rudder still works, but very slow to respond."

Jason peered over the stern at the rudder and saw the wood was split and half was missing. If she hit it again, what remained would be gone, so the captain had Jib bring his spear to monitor the back of the boat.

In the crow's nest, Aiden's continued search for the shadow of the serpent was briefly interrupted when he caught a glimpse of Aetna, the volcano Scota had described to him. It was larger than he expected with a thin band of smoke, venting from the crater-shaped peak. The majestic mountain was impressive and imposing. Looking back to the water, a dark image appeared, encroaching on the back of the ship.

"There!" the blacksmith shouted, pointing north.

Hondo went back to join Jib. Nothing was visible, but they stood at the ready. For some reason, the sea dragon raised its tail out of the water, slapping the surface on its way down. It felt as if she was trying to get their attention and it worked, but they were determined the monster wouldn't claim the Argo if they could get a clear shot. The crew was becoming impatient too. They'd rather face her and get it over with than play a waiting game.

The tail broke the surface again, this time revealing a section of the back as the creature rolled along, heading on a collision course. Then her heads broke the surface, all six of them, driving the crew backward in astonishment. The serpent put her front legs on the rear railing. It was hard to tell if she was pushing down or trying to climb aboard or maybe both.

Jib was the first to react, tossing his spear in the eye of one of her heads, causing the monster to recoil from the painful strike. Hondo's splintered oar penetrated the neck of a second head. She was wounded, but neither impact would bring about her death. The creature became furious and tried to remove the spears, but they were buried too deep. One of the Argonauts was knocked down and two went overboard. She paid them no mind as they splashed about the cold water; she wanted the Argo now more than ever.

There was a panicked confusion that swept over the crew. The sea dragon would surely swamp the ship if they didn't do something and fast. Jib ran below deck, grabbed three oil lamps, and hastily rushed back. He tossed each, one after another, at the serpent, all making direct hits. The candles had been extinguished by earlier crashing waves, and no remaining oil lamps were lit. Jib needed a flame for an arrow, but there was none.

Aiden watched the serpent's attempt to ravage the stern. He too, realized they needed a flame. Instinctively, he pulled out the ruby necklace and aimed it at the beast, hoping his idea would work. The rocking of the ship made it difficult to keep the red ray focused in one spot. He tried to adjust the beam of the necklace with the movement of the Argo as another sailor went overboard.

The situation was getting desperate when the serpent suddenly burst into flames as did the Argo. The ray of the ruby had served its purpose, igniting the oil, but setting the ship on fire was unexpected. With its heads on fire, the creature plunged back in the water in its attempt to extinguish the inferno. She thrashed wildly in the waves, forcing water to crash against the stern, putting out the fire aboard ship before sinking out of sight.

Argo's crew retrieved the men from the sea, cautiously on the lookout for Scylla at the same time. Aiden couldn't tell where she'd vanished to, and the fear of the creature's return was with everyone. Men encompassed the deck armed with bows while Atalanta paced back and forth, midship, armed with her own. She was the fiercest of hunters, even among men, and the bow was her specialty.

They waited in anticipation of another attack as the ship continued to sail south. When it became apparent they were safe, the hull was struck again, rocking the vessel and their confidence. They remained on high alert, but the creature never returned.

The Argo and the crew had luckily survived every destructive challenge they'd faced. Whether it was fate or an act of the gods, they were alive. Their egos were out of control, and they would certainly celebrate when the ship reached port.

Standing at the mirror, the princess was glad the stress of the day was over. She felt drained and ready to return to the castle. Her man was alive, still on his quest for the feather that would bind them together forever.

"Don't think you can view the mirror every time you knock," the wizard said with assurance.

"And why not?"

"Because we both have better things to do. You can't spend all your time in front of the glass and still live your life."

"I know you're right, Edric, but right now, Aiden is my world. There is a connection between us I can't explain. Life will never be normal until he returns to me. I will be back and I promise not to be a pest, but while he's gone, I have to do something or I'll lose my sanity."

"Well, we don't want him returning to a crazy woman, do we?"

"No, right now his world is complicated enough. He should return to a woman of compassion and strength."

Twice Sail to Phaeacia

With the deadly passage behind them and conquered, the ship would need the rudder fixed before they could resume their voyage to the Phaeacian Islands. The Argo dropped anchor in shallow water and lowered the sails while two carpenters worked on the repair.

"Why is it we don't port in Thrinacia? It's so close," Aiden asked of Jason.

"Three reasons. The volcano has the power to blow up the island and everything in sight by the will of the gods. Helios grazes his sacred cattle of the sun there, they can't be touched by humans in any way. Odysseus found that out the hard way, and lastly, this side of the island has no ports."

"No ports is all you had to say, but what did Odysseus learn the hard way?"

"Helios had seven herds of cattle and seven herds of sheep, fifty in each. They didn't breed or become fewer in number. Odysseus told his men they couldn't touch the herds of the sun god in any way and avoid them at all cost. In their hunger, they chose to ignore his warning and slaughtered some of the cattle. On their way to Phaeacia, Zeus struck the ship with a lightning bolt, killing all men aboard, except for the captain. Odysseus was able the swim to the shores of Phaeacia."

"So far, my quest has been filled with the most extraordinary tales and adventures one could ever imagine. How far to the Phaeacian Islands?"

"About four to five days, depending on the wind."

Once the rudder was repaired and the sails raised, the Argo began its eastern voyage around the sole of the boot. With a strong wind, the ship reached the heel in two days, with only the Adriatiki Sea separating them from the Greek mainland about three days away.

With Jason and Medea planning to wed once they arrived in Greece, the crew was busy making the Argo shipshape. The boat was scrubbed from stern to stern and fresh paint applied where needed to make a first-class royal impression. It had been some time since the crew had been to a large port with good food, drink, and women. Anticipation and morale were high with thoughts of getting back to the real world.

What appeared to be a simple crossing of the sea soon turned out to be nothing of the sort. High winds made controlling the Argo's course very difficult, if not impossible. On the first day, the ship sailed in a large circle, making no progress at all. The next two days weren't much better, although they were halfway across the span of water.

Jason gathered the crew together. Their morale had been deflated by the lack of progress and unending course rotation, but what he had to say wouldn't improve their outlook.

"Men, the gods are controlling the wind. Which gods I can't say with any certainty, but they are persistent in thwarting our crossing. The wind sets our heading and steers our path, how long it endures, I know not. We have food and water for five days, which may not be enough, so rationing our supply is mandatory and in everyone's best interest."

The crew wasn't surprised by the action, but the announcement raised doubts about reaching Greece at all. Mortals had no power over the gods, and the ship could wander endlessly until discharged from their grasp.

Two more days at sea and nothing had changed. Even the birds were nonexistent, unable to fly in such weather. The tempest remained harsh with the crew staying below deck as much as possible. The sails were stretched beyond their ability by the constant change in the wind's direction, raising questions about potential destruction of the fabric. Without sails, the wind wouldn't power the Argo, leaving the men no choice but to row for the distant coast. The feat would be demanding with rations, but it might be the only way out of their dilemma.

The ship's fate was in the hands of a higher power for an unknown purpose, and the gods had a reputation of manipulating the endurance of mortals with their competitive nature. It was a game and a test of willpower, designed to humor the deity.

Another two days on this course and the food and water were gone. The crew resorted to taping a keg of wine from the hold for refreshment, which enhanced their stamina while easing their frustration. With no food in their stomach, there was little tolerance for the intoxicating beverage, although it made for a much happier, forbearing crew.

Jason hailed Theseus to his cabin after some thought, deciding the crow's nest needed to be manned despite the conditions. He wasn't pleased with riding out the storm from such a high position, even when the captain said to tie himself to the mast. Jason told the Argonaut to blow the ship's horn if he spied land, and the ship would drop its sails and break out the oars. Periclymenus would relieve him every eight hours, leaving the nest empty at night.

As he departed, wind howled through the cabin, snuffing out the candles, as it had every time the door was opened. Medea was tired of relighting the candles, but since the oil lamps were used to fight off the sea dragon, she had no other choice.

A new day blows and there's still no sign of land or birds. The prospects for the ship and crew were becoming desperate. At one point, the Argo's circle was so tight; it cut through its own wake, and there were worries the ship could flounder and sink. Medea had been praying to the gods for assistance, over the days, with no response, and Aiden began to wonder if he'd ever reach Egypt.

On the ninth day, hunger was becoming the monster for even the strongest of men, sapping their strength and disrupting their thought. With the waters too rough to fish and no birds in the sky, they were at the mercy of the deities, hoping one would listen and come to their aid. Life aboard ship had become a miserable existence.

"Land ho!" came the cry from the crow's nest.

"Land ho!" the echo from the prow.

Hondo rushed to the cabin and informed the captain, blowing out the candles for a countless time. Jason went on deck and ordered the sails lowered and oars at the ready. He pulled his eyeglass once he reached the bow, relieved by the sight and motioned Theseus down from the mast.

Fighting the wind and the sails was a deadly task with two getting tangled in the ropes and several nearly thrown or blown overboard. The wind died down instantly, cutting the ship's speed in half. The Argo had bested the gods for now, and they knew if the sails were raised again, the gust would only return. The water remained rough for the weakened crew to tread with the wave surge, but they fought through the stomach pains and focused on reaching the shore and kissing the ground.

The crew had to stop many times on their way to the shore without the stamina and their energy spent. The wind gave them no trouble along the coastline as they finally reached the islands. One sail was raised to facilitate their arrival at port on the nearest island of Scheria. All the islands supported lush green meadows and large orchards.

Once the port came into view, they saw a city painted in white and a fleet of ships docked. On the small rise behind the city was a circular wall, with a small entrance, encompassing the royal palace of King Alcinous and Queen Arete. The palace had a roof shining like silver with golden columned porches.

The Argo found a place to dock, and the crew debarked for the marketplace, with appetites ready to satisfy. When Jason reached the end of the dock, he noticed the marketplace was surrounded by the dark-skinned Colchian army and hastily called back his men for their protection and that of the ship. No wonder the port was so full, they weren't merchant ships.

The Colchians moved closer, but still maintained a safe yet threatening distance and demanded Medea and the fleece be turned over to them. Jason refused their demands as the priestess and Atalanta escaped down the shore to skirt the army and reach the palace. The Argonauts boarded the Argo and moved the ship out of the port to the far end of the island.

When Medea reached the palace, Atalanta stood guard, and she entered to address the queen. Arete sat near the hearth at her loom, spinning silver thread. She looked very stately in her white floor-length gown and was about the same age.

"My lady, I beg you to receive me and hear my request."

Arete rose from her loom and greeted the visitor face to face. Her eyes were clear, like one with understanding, and she wore a thin white veil. Medea fell to her knees before the monarch and began to tell her story. She told of fleeing her father, King Aeetes, because she fell in love with Jason, their acquisition of the fleece, and the murder of her brother, the captain of the Colchian fleet. Medea pleaded and prayed through her tears for the queen to protect them from the great force of Colchians in the harbor.

The queen, moved by a sincere request from the impending queen of Lolcus and potential royal equal, went to her garden and pleaded Medea's case to her husband, Alcinous.

"Husband, if the Colchians are given Medea, it will lead to her bitter doom. She has been cleansed for her brother's death, came to Phaeacia to wed, and the Golden Fleece has already been won by Jason. Medea has broken my heart with her tears and you must not give in to the Colchian demands."

"Aeetes's kingdom is strong, although far away. If I don't comply, his army could war upon us."

His queen pleaded once more on Medea's behalf and reminded the king that a marriage would create a new ally in Lolcus.

Alcinous left the garden and entered the chamber where the priestess still kneeled. He lifted her up from her stoop and promised his protection as best he could. The king escorted

Medea to his chariot and delivered her back to the seashore where he drove his team between the opposing forces.

The Colchians made their case for the surrender of the fleece and return of the princess to her father's court. The king considered their request, but drove his chariot to the Argonaut line and took Jason's hand, admiring the fleece and received them to the city before he spoke.

"I will determine if Medea be a maiden. If she is, I will give her to you, but if she is no longer a virgin, I will deny your request. I will give you my answer tomorrow."

The Colchian army seemed satisfied and pulled back. Jason, though, was concerned, not having consummated his love for Medea. The Argonauts followed the king's chariot back to the palace where they were welcomed by the people, bearing gifts of garments, sheep, and calves along with jars of wine and honey. The princess was given fine linen and jewelry. They attended a reception in their honor where Jason and Medea kneeled and thanked the monarchs for securing their safety and protection.

The queen whispered words of thanks in the king's ear and shared her idea to resolve the predicament facing the court. She urged the pair to rise before announcing her decision.

"Medea, have you consummated your relationship with Jason?"

"No, Your Highness, the proper time and place has eluded us."

"Well then, you leave me no choice. You must wed and consummate your marriage tonight."

"That would be our wish."

"Your wedding will be performed in the sacred cave of Makris, and when you return, you will no longer be a virgin or of any further interest of the Colchians."

"We thank you both for your blessing."

"We must find something appropriate for the occasion. Come with me."

The queen and the princess went to her chambers to search for a dress, something fitting in white. While Medea was willing to settle on several choices, the queen was set on perfection. Once the ultimate selection was made, the princess bathed and applied sensuous fragrances to her skin. Arete sent her maiden to the garden for fresh flowers as she combed Medea's long hair.

Jason's attire, dark pants and white shirt, was provided by the villagers since he and the king were of different stature. He showered rather than bathed, then returned to the palace to wait on his beloved.

When the maiden returned from the garden, she made two bouquets and a floral garland. Arete helped Medea with her wedding dress, veil, and garland before leading her to a floor-length mirror for her final approval. The princess was pleased, feeling sensual and pleasing for her man while reflecting the modesty of a virgin.

Jason was astonished upon Medea's return. She was radiant and beautiful in a way he'd never seen her before. Their eyes were glued to each other as she sauntered to join his side, handing Atalanta the second bouquet on her way. The huntress was surprised by the gesture, this being her first wedding occasion of memory and not exactly the image of a lady.

The ceremonial march to the sacred cave was led by the king and queen, followed by the priest and maidens tossing white daisies at the feet of the wedding couple. The entourage of Argonauts and villagers stretched out behind them.

The path to the cave passed by a fragrant meadow of wildflowers before reaching a dense stand of trees cut by a stream. The water flowed from the large mouth of the cave, over the shiny rocks and through surrounding fragrant bushes. The sound of the torrent breaking over the rocks was peaceful and relaxing.

Inside the sweet-smelling grotto, the priest took his place behind a stone altar and lit two wide white candles. While the monarchs stood on one side and the huntress on the other, Jason realized he'd not selected his best man. He turned to meet his band of Argonauts, looking for the one most suitable, consciously unable to select a member of his crew without causing hard feelings. Instead, he quietly asked Aiden if he would do the honors while secretly handing him the ring. The blacksmith took his place next to the huntress as they exchanged awkward looks.

"Don't say a word," she whispered.

"I'm just as shocked as you to be standing here."

The rushed ceremony began, and when it was time to surrender the ring, Aiden pulled out the Rhinegold ring by mistake and handed it to the groom, who handed it back. Flushed and embarrassed, he quickly corrected his error, which was met by the captain's huge grin.

Sealed with a kiss, they were finally husband and wife, acknowledged by the noisy outburst from the crew. Villagers provided wine outside the cave for the numerous toasts before everyone returned to the palace for a feast. The maidens took trays of fruit and meat, resting them around the edges of the altar, tossed more cut flowers about, and then, were the last to leave.

Alone at last, Jason spread the fleece out, over the surface of the stone altar and stood watching his wife slowly and teasingly remove her clothing. She studied the expression on his face with her sultry seduction. He'd never seen her naked before; her radiant natural beauty left him speechless. He'd had erotic dreams about Medea, and now, his dreams were becoming truth. Jason knew he was a very lucky man and refused to take it for granted.

The groom admired her ample white breasts as he too removed his garments, although not as seductively as she. Their lustful eyes met and slowly worked their way down the curves and muscles of the other's torso and back up again, stopping briefly at the pubic region before regaining their lover's stare. Their anticipation was overwhelming.

Jason took Medea up in his arms and carried her to the altar, gently placing her on the fleece and lying at her side. Their hands exploring while feeding each other grapes, occasionally smashing one on the other and smearing the sweet juice all over their skin. Touching and tasting each other was an intensely sensitive and extremely erotic experience, best savored at a leisurely pace. Their romantic interlude continued until their sweat became fluid, and the lovers' shared nectar left them spent. Exhausted, they fell asleep in a lover's grip.

When the married couple awoke, they dressed, folded up the fleece, and walked back down the mountain trail, holding hands, arriving at the palace where the boisterous celebration feast was still going on. Drink flowed freely while maidens taunted their rowdy guests with flirtatious entertainment. There was a disruptive round of applause as they entered, followed by a comment from the Phaeacian queen, loud enough for all in attendance to hear.

"The Colchians won't want you now, my dear, you're spoiled goods."

"I may be a defiant daughter, but I'm not a reluctant wife. Love conquers all."

"Indeed."

The remarks caused a great outburst of laughter, followed by condolences and sympathy at her father's expense. Jason, too, found himself the target of misplaced humor by his men. The celebration went on for hours until the food was gone, wine spent, and the partiers passed out.

In the morning, the hungover Egyptians, with Aiden, walked back toward the harbor. They noticed several of the Colchian ships had left the port, leaving the merchant ships to dominate the early activity on the docks. From the marketplace, they could count the vessels, including the Argo.

"Today we seek a ship to carry us home, but chances are we won't find one willing to sail all the way to the Celt Island. I doubt any of these ships have ever ventured past the Pillars of Hercules," Jib shared.

"So what happens if you can't find one?" Aiden asked.

"Then we won't have any choice. We'll have to continue on to Egypt. Maybe the pharaoh will see fit to provide us a vessel on Meritaten's behalf, or we'll have to find a boat of our own. Either way, we have to sail ourselves back home."

"Life gets complicated sometimes, doesn't it?"

"Simple is never easy."

"Let's ask the merchants and then we'll know for sure. I'd prefer we travel on together, besides, finding my way around Egypt would be much easier with you than without."

The travelers ventured to the Argo, surprisingly berthed between two enemy ships with members of their army walking the docks to the shore. From the few ships that remained, they went to receive their answer from the king. Just like the day before, the two sides lined up, facing each other, dressed for a kill. Even though the Argonauts were vastly outnumbered, on this day, they were armed to the teeth. They weren't intimidated by the numbers and remained a dangerous and formidable foe.

Word spread fast, all the way to the palace, as the crowd grew. This time the king arrived on his chariot armed with a small force of soldiers to back him up. He drove his chariot to the center of the standoff and stepped out, facing the Colchians.

"I have determined that the princess is no maiden and she has wed. Therefore, I deny your request she be returned. Also, Jason has won the right to possess the fleece through his courage, so I deny that request as well."

There was an eerie silence before the Colchians backed away and dispersed. The clash was over before it ever started, and the Argo was finally free. King Aeetes wouldn't be happy with the outcome this day, but he'd have to work though the frustration himself.

Jason thanked the king once more for his protection and hospitality, advising his departure within the week. The king invited the newlywed couple to the palace for dinner until the day they leave.

"Prince and princess, king and queen, both should dine together."

"Thank you, sire, we gratefully oblige."

"I guess I should've said king and king since you claim your rightful title to the throne when you reach Lolcus."

"That's true."

The gathering moved to the docks where it was already busy. Jib worked his way from ship to ship, trying to enlist their services. In each case, none of the options were tangible. Jason was observing their progress until they reached his berth.

"What's wrong with the Argo? She's a fine ship."

"You're headed for Lolcus, us to Crete."

"Yeah, but she'd still get you closer than you are now, besides, she sails to Crete after Lolcus."

"We'll keep that in mind, don't leave without us."

It was getting late in the morning when horns sounded in the marketplace. Villagers and sailors alike were concentrating on the square. Music filled the air, and Orpheus ran by with his lyre in hand. No one could resist the draw of song, leaving the docks entirely empty.

The event was like a talent show. Musicians, singers, and dancers, all interacting with each other. Orpheus was in heaven, on a stage, surrounded by those of his kind. Villagers began delivering more gifts to the Argonauts as if they were immortal. After some time, games and magic took over the stage. Aiden noticed the king and queen were mixing with the crowd and taking part in the festivities. They reflected the vision the blacksmith had of himself, once he were royalty.

Aiden's study of the monarchs was interrupted by the sound of something popping in pots, hanging over two large fires. The popping became more rapid by the moment and his curiosity got the best of him. He had to find out what it was. Soon, the pots were removed from the flame and the white puffy contents emptied into bowls. The first to arrive were the children, using both hands to fill their mouths and pockets. They were dancing and skipping all around the square. Whatever it was, it was like gold to them.

"What do you call this?" Aiden asked a vendor as he tasted the treat.

"Popcorn."

"And what is popcorn?"

"Dried kernels of corn," the vendor replied very politely, though looking at the blacksmith as if he was dim-witted.

He watched the entire process, pleased he had a new idea to take home if he ever got there. The sea salt and garlic butter was a nice touch too, except for the gritty, greasy hands, though popcorn was fun and very filling. The treat was definitely worth the mess.

After a time, storytelling became the focus of the day, with all sitting down except for the teller. The king was telling his story as Aiden found a seat. A tale of Odysseus, his visit to Phaeacia, and the shipwreck when he lost his entire crew. The queen went next with a story about her great-grandfather Poseidon and his chariot pulled by seahorses.

When she had finished, the queen welcomed Jason to the platform. He shared the tale of the dragon guarding the Golden Fleece. Medea told stories of Heracles's courage. Atalanta shared her fully armed footrace with suitors, which she won. After several recounts, the burden fell on Aiden. He shared his encounter with the Rhinegold Maidens and the dwarf king. The stories seemed to be the most popular activity of the day, especially for the children who also participated.

The Phaeacians were a tight-knit culture, comfortable with their simple lives and confident with their place in the world. They were a happy people and very generous hosts. Again, he thought about what he could take back with him, and storytelling would make his list as he was already living many adventures worth sharing.

The next couple days showed no improvement in transportation to Crete. Two ships departed for Athens, one to the Balearic Islands, and the last to Malta. Aiden considered Malta as did the Egyptians, but both decided a busier port would better serve their needs. The next morning, two merchant ships did arrive, one from Crete and the other from the Balearic's. They called on the captain of the Crete vessel and made their arrangements, but their departure was three days out with cargo transfers.

They passed by the Argo to let Jason know their transport was achieved and found the Argonauts sailed that day. All were sorry, they had to part company, but it was inevitable after all. The captain wished Aiden well on his quest. They were joined by Queen Arete who was escorting Medea to the Argo. They paid their respects, and the monarch had some parting advice for the princess.

"Forget your witchery and enchantments, my dear, never practice against the life of anyone again. You will soon be queen. Queens, unlike their husbands, must be stately and dignified. We are the nurturers of the people, the kingdom, and the conscience of the king."

Medea acknowledged her words, realizing the queen was the woman that Circe had prophesied. Her advice was wisdom, well spoken and from the heart. She boarded the Argo and the queen returned to the palace. With the cargo loaded and crew aboard, they watched the ship sail away.

Jib tapped Aiden on the shoulder and pointed to the recent Balearic arrival.

"Isn't that Tobias?"

"It is."

The blacksmith had dreaded a run-in with the notoriously dangerous contender of Ariana's hand. He wondered what his adversary was doing here, but wasn't about to ask. As Tobias walked the docks to the market, their eyes met. At first, the rival looked surprised, but his expression quickly changed to repugnance. Aiden wasn't afraid of Tobias and, at the same time, knew confrontation wasn't the answer. With both on the same island, it would be impossible to avoid each other.

When Aiden was in the marketplace with the Egyptians, Tobias kept tabs on the blacksmith while maintaining his distance. He had two manservant's at his side, in their twenties, that weren't with him on the docks. Both had rugged exteriors with a swagger of arrogance that worsened with the consumption of alcohol. With a show of muscle and lack of intimidation, the two approached Aiden in the company of his escorts.

"Sailing with the Cretans would be a mistake."

"How's that?" Aiden asked, not backing down.

"Let's just say it's a long voyage and accidents can happen."

"So are you two the mouth of Tobias? Can't he speak for himself?"

"We're only offering generous advice, friend."

"I'm not your friend and you can tell Tobias I'm not pressured by his threats. If anyone takes another ship, it should be he."

"So be it. We've given you the message, the choice is yours to make."

Aiden watched the two intimidators work their way back through the crowd. They had words with Tobias who didn't look pleased by the conversation. He stared back at the blacksmith with a scowl on his face, and the three walked away from the market.

"This could be an interesting voyage," Jib surmised.

"Very interesting and very dangerous."

"Not to worry, Aiden, we've got your back," Hondo added.

Over the next two days, the competitors had no contact. It was as if they had fallen off the face of the earth. They were less of a threat when Aiden knew where they were, and now he wondered what the three were plotting. Something was awry, he could feel it.

It was their last night in Phaeacia. They visited the palace and thanked the monarchs for their generosity and kindness. While they dined, the king told Aiden of another feather seeker who had arrived two days prior.

"Does he know his destination?"

"Not at first, but he asked a lot of questions. He knows he has to find the temple at Heliopolis, that's about all. Can I expect more visitors on the quest?"

"Only if they're lost and don't know where to go, or like us, our transportation brought us through your port."

The king described the competitor for the feather as a tall middle-aged man with long blond hair and with callused hands. Aiden recalled the man, but he wasn't from any of the local villages. The king hadn't seen the seeker all day, and Aiden hadn't seen him at all. To the blacksmith's surprise, the king went with them to the inn at the market for parting mugs of wine. Tobias walked to their table and stood next to Aiden.

"Sire, gentlemen, tomorrow we sail. May we all celebrate a blameless night."

"What does that mean?" the king asked as the Celt walked away.

"I believe that was a threat, directed at me," Aiden stated.

"I'll have my men keep an eye on him tonight."

Rising from the tables, about an hour later, the king returned to the palace and the men went upstairs to their second-story rooms. In the morning, they would meet at the docks.

The Egyptians arrived, one after another, to the harbor, waiting on the blacksmith. The longer they waited, the closer it came to launch. They checked his empty room and the marketplace, with no trace. They returned to the ship to face Tobias and noticed the blond contender was also aboard.

"Have you seen Aiden?" Jib asked.

"What have you done with him?" Dak accused.

"Is he missing?"

"You know he's missing. Where is he?"

"You affront me, gentlemen, I don't take kindly to insults. If you lost him, go find him."

They never boarded the ship, choosing to search for their friend, with the villagers and the palace guards help. The search went on for three days. Nothing turned up, and no one had seen him that morning. The Egyptians finally decided to take the next boat home, sensing the end of the blacksmith's quest.

Aiden was awakened by a bucket of cold seawater.

"Wake up. We're here," the Balearic captain advised the sleeping passenger.

"Where am I?"

"At your destination."

"Sir, if I knew where that was, I wouldn't ask."

"The Balearic Islands, you paid for the passage."

"I paid?"

"Well, your friends did. They said you had a bit too much to drink and wanted to make sure you didn't miss your voyage home."

"How many days passed?"

"Four."

"And you didn't think that was strange. No one stays drunk for four days. I was drugged."

"Sorry, sir, we had no idea. I'll help find you a return ship."

"You do that. I'm getting something to eat."

Tobias was responsible, no doubt, at the hands of his two servants. Aiden was angry, but worse, he could be dead. He wondered why they didn't just kill him. Was there a purpose for leaving him alive? Arrangements were made for an afternoon departure, and the blacksmith was on his way back to Phaeacia. Tobias would have a head start of more than a week, enough time to reach Heliopolis and possibly find the feather. The voyage was a depressing one and feelings of betrayal and loss were haunting.

When Aiden made port, he couldn't believe his eyes. Hondo was standing near a merchant vessel. Once the ship was berthed, he walked up to the Egyptian.

"Miss me?"

"You're still alive. Thank the gods. We feared the worst."

The friends walked back to the market and joined the others. They sat at a table and shared the experiences of the last eight days. Aiden notified the king, but there was no way to prove Tobias was involved.

Intimidation of Lilith

It was a good feeling to finally be aboard a ship to Crete along with his comrades. The blacksmith couldn't stop thinking about the two men ahead of him. Before, he had no idea where he stood, but now he did. He wished he knew more about the mysterious blond. Whoever he was, the man was threat enough to make it this far in the quest on his own, something the blacksmith wasn't sure he could have accomplished.

"Crete is ruled by King Minos and his wife, Queen Pasiphae. Their palace at Knossos is five levels high, with thirteen hundred rooms, built in a labyrinth. The maze was a killing ground for the Minotaur to hunt young sacrificial victims until it was slain by Theseus," the Minoan captain shared with his passengers.

"Theseus of Athens?" Aiden asked.

"The very same. Athens sent seven young men and women as sacrifices to the Minotaur in order to avoid war with King Minos. Theseus pretended to be a victim and became a hero of the Athenians."

"We traveled with him aboard the Argo. He shared little about his exploits."

"He wasn't a braggart."

"A Minotaur, what is it?" Jib joined the conversation.

"Asterion, the bull of Minos and the son of Queen Pasiphae. He was half-man with the head and tail of a bull. You'll see the Minoans worship the bull with dance and architecture as soon as we arrive in port. The image is everywhere."

As they sailed along the coast of Crete, the land had fields of sheep, thousands in number, and few standing trees. The enormous Temple of Knossos came into view long before reaching the harbor. The closer they sailed, the more spectacular its presence. The port city was larger than anything the blacksmith had seen so far. Multilevel buildings dominated the skyline with colorful columns and clerestory windows.

The harbor moored countless ships of different origin, surrounded by warehouses. Once the Cretan vessel berthed, they easily found passage with another ship sailing to Egypt the next day. Walking the docks to the shore, the group took a peek inside one of the warehouses. There were thousands of terracotta vases, some standing upright, others on their side, separated by location. Containers were moved in and out at a constant pace, monitored by workers at each site.

"What's in all the vases?" Jib asked one of the men guarding the exterior door.

"We have olives, dried fish, beans, grain, wine, and olive oil going out. Wheat, corn, wine, beer, raisins, nuts, and lamp oil, inbound. Are you loading or unloading?"

"Neither, I was just curious."

Moving on, the active marketplace was anchored by a large fountain, a new sight to the Celt. Some vendors were set up on the busy street with their products trailing into the shops. Residents filled jugs with water from spigots mounted on several exterior walls. Women wore short-sleeved garments with strapless bodices open at the navel, and men wore kilts or loincloths. They were dark-skinned people, more so than the Colchians.

Frescos of bulls, full body and head only, were painted inside and out of the structures. Horns were mounted over doorways and from roof peaks, just as the captain had described. One large painting depicted a scene of the bull dance.

The palace sat back off the harbor, with its columns of red and massive size that was unfathomable at least to the blacksmith. Even the homes surrounding the palace were large, some two levels high. An elaborate aqueduct brought water into the city, and some areas had multiple outdoor oil lamps on pillars of wood. Horse-drawn wagons staged along the side of the palace were being loaded with clay containers.

Walking back toward the harbor, they stopped at several shops along the way. One of the most impressive was a gem shop. The varieties of brilliant colors were radiant in the light and could be set in rings or necklaces on site. Two well-dressed buyers were picking through the baskets and selecting stones of the highest quality.

"Jib?" a voice uttered from behind.

The Egyptian turned, surprised to hear his name called out in a foreign land. The voice was that of Seth, the pharaoh's buyer of precious stones. The two had a history with Jib's ties to the royal family.

"Seth, I guess I don't need to ask what brings you here."

"No, but what are you doing in Crete? The pharaoh thinks you're dead."

"As you can see, I'm not."

"What of Meritaten and Gaytheios?"

"They're alive and well."

Jib related the details of their departure to his astounded friend who in return shared news from their homeland. King Akhenaten had moved the royal palace from Thebes to Amarna in an effort to diminish the power of the priests over his own choice of deity. The two made arrangements for Jib's entourage to sail aboard the pharaoh's ship on their return to Egypt. It would add one more day's wait, but well worth the delay.

Aiden browsed the massive gem selection. He wanted to find something special to signify his devotion to Ariana. He collected a handful of jewels before settling on a light pink amethyst, which he had made into a ring. Hopefully, a wedding ring, but the gem would make a fine gift, even if he lost the quest.

The pottery shop next door displayed plates, cups, and bowls with brilliant bands of red and blue colors, some with embedded stones. Vases of various sizes, with or without handles, were painted with images of the bull, olive trees, as well as men and women performing diverse tasks. An array of figurines with topless females in bell-shaped skirts, men wearing nothing but a codpiece, and blue dolphins were scattered about. The mural walls exhibited bronze sun disks with a blue-green patina, inlaid with golden symbols of the sun, full moon, and crescent moon. The craftsmanship and detail of the shop were extraordinary.

The city had shops for everything produced locally in the many factories, along with a district dedicated to imports from around the world of the inland sea. If you couldn't find what you wanted, it probably didn't exist.

A religious procession worked its way from the palace and down the street toward the market, attracting a gathering as it moved along. Priests, both men and women, wore long gowns of light fabric followed by two men wearing terracotta masks in the image of a bull, with the long-horned animal in tow. It was apparent the bull dance was about take place once the procession reached its destination, and Aiden wasn't going to miss the event.

Somehow as the following grew in size, the blacksmith became separated from Jib and the others. He wasn't even sure if they were among the emergent spectators as the multitude reached a vacant square, spreading out to create a very large opening at the center. A short religious ceremony ensued, in a foreign tongue, blessing the bull, with onlookers placing their fists at the corners of their foreheads.

The first challenger of the dance, wearing the mask, grabbed the furthest span of the bull's horns and was instantly thrown over the animal's head, landing awkwardly on his back. Aiden's first thought, as the man scrambled to his feet, was why this was called a dance at all. The craziness went on as one after another took the challenge until one participant landed on his feet and it was over. They celebrated the apparent winner, and he got to keep the mask he wore, like a trophy.

The procession moved on, making a loop around the marketplace, until they reached a rectangular stone altar at the back side of the temple. The offering table, covered with the gifts of the seasonal harvest, was painted with bull images and horns mounted on either end. Another prayer ceremony was conducted, followed by the sacrifice of the bull to the gods. The animal was carried to a nearby table, encompassed by a trough, and slaughtered in preparation of a sacred meal. The blood of the bull was collected as much as possible for some other religious rite or purpose.

In a distance grove, the blacksmith saw olives being harvested and decided to get a closer look. Pickers were dropping the green fruit from ladders into large nets. The green olives were hard and not like those he'd tasted at the market. These had a bitter taste, and he wondered how they processed them into an edible product.

He noticed a crow, sitting atop a tree, a couple rows away. Aiden studied the bird as its image seemed to expand and contract, revealing a faint outline of something much larger; a woman. He knew his shape-shifting vision was that of Lilith, spying on his progress. The blacksmith approached the tree, avoiding eye contact with the crow until he was close enough to hold a conversation.

"Lilith, I see you for who you are."

The blackbird took flight, landing on the ground several rows away, where the harvest was complete. Aiden followed her movement and was astonished when she took her feminine form. She was as beautiful as he'd been told, with her golden hair, pale skin, and rose-red lips. The queen of the dark, goddess of magic, and seductress witch took a lustful stance, barely clothed, and he could feel the power in her soul.

"Now you see me for the woman I am, standing before you, in the flesh."

"I could see you before."

"Only a faint image, Aiden, not the real me."

"What is it you want from me?"

"When you escaped the sweet song of Lorelei, I thought it was just luck. Then you were able to avoid the enchantment of my Rhinegold Maidens, and I knew you had the power of magic cast over your head, like a halo. My maidens revealed secrets better kept to themselves, and as a result, you were able to steal my ring away from Alberich, not too surprising, considering he can be quite inept at times. I realized you could see more of me than you should in the delta. You, blacksmith, have more than one spell protecting your life and guiding your quest. *I want my ring back!*"

"I'll give it back, in trade for a feather of the phoenix."

"A feather won't attain the love you seek. Love is but an abomination of submissive, self-gratifying dominance, one over the other. It will only leave you disheartened, discouraged, and dejected."

"I'm not disillusioned like you. The anguish and torment that you speak would only haunt me if I don't acquire the feather. My offer is still valid."

"The ring is not yours to trade."

"It is right now."

"Who has cast this magic, which gives you the poise to be so impudent?"

"I believe you meant confidence. I say not the source of my power unlike your maidens."

"I want my ring back!"

"It's yours in trade, very simple, or is it that you can't acquire a feather to barter for what you desire?"

"I don't barter with mortals. I destroy them first."

"Now you're letting your pride rule over your judgment."

"Don't test my powers, young man, you're no match for me."

"Oh, but I am. You would have already destroyed me and taken what you want, if it weren't so."

"I will win. I'll make you regret your misguided insolence for an eternity."

"Why can't we both win? What is so difficult about this transaction if we both get what we want?"

"Because both the feather and the ring already belong to me."

"If you change your mind, I should be easy for you to find."

"You'll never be able to hide from the reach of my influence and power, I'll have my way."

"Maybe so, but you can't hide from me either."

"You will feel, with fear, the pain in my wrath."

"It's a shame that a woman with such beauty can be so bitter."

Aiden turned his back on Lilith and walked away. He felt vulnerable, but did his best not to show it. The blacksmith was sure they would meet again, and hopefully, the queen of the dark underworld would have a change of heart. He was fortunate to have the protection of Edric's magic; without the spells, he would've been helpless against her powers.

The wizard, observing the confrontation through the mirror, had matched wits with the witch and remained anonymous. She would never be able to find the ring, with the spell of invisibility cast upon it. Aiden had handled himself well, a little testy, but confident and unafraid. There was no need to tell Ariana, so he'd keep it to himself, at least for now.

Edric decided to check on Scota's progress and rode out to the coast. It was a beautiful day until he arrived. She was gone, and he felt sad having missed her, hoping maybe he'd see her again once she was settled. On his way back, he rode up on the king and prince, who were headed toward the coast.

"Sire."

"Wizard."

"Are you riding to Scota's?"

"We are."

"She has already fled."

They were halfway back to the castle before Darian began to ask any further questions of the wizard.

"What can you say about the quest?"

"Nothing much to tell, really."

"What of Aiden?"

"He's doing well, it's a shame you couldn't just let the two marry."

"You know I couldn't do that without controversy."

"I do, it's too bad we chose a quest so difficult."

Aiden returned to the marketplace and tried to find his friends without any success. He began to ask the outdoor vendors, one after another, before he finally found one who could answer.

"I saw them walking the trail to Arkalochori with a woman."

"What is Arkalochori?"

"A sacred Minoan cave."

"How far away?"

"Twenty miles to the south, but I'd ride a horse."

"Right."

Aiden wondered if Lilith could react so fast, but there was no other reasonable explanation for the woman leading them away. It was an assumption based on the theory they were being led, and she wasn't another siren. He expected to find the Egyptians before they reached the cave but that didn't happen. He considered they may have taken another path somewhere else.

He stood at the mouth of the sacred cave, deciding to go in and look around, even though they weren't there. Large chunks of the cave's ceiling had collapsed to the floor below, challenging his detailed investigation of the first cave. Painted colored images filled the walls. More blue dolphins and black bulls with some new ones as well; fish, sheep, and olive trees. The walls had a strange festival appeal. The collapse had blocked two smaller openings on one side, making them impassable, but three on the left were unaffected.

He was speechless as he entered the side chamber. The wall, on one side, was lined with hundreds of bronze axes, along with twenty-five gold ones and seven silver. The opposite side had stacks of bronze long swords and a stone altar piled with daggers. The stockpile of weapons was offensive not defensive blades and made no sense stashed twenty miles from the port.

Did they belong to the Minoans since it was their sacred cave or someone else? The idea the weapons were Minoan seemed unlikely since they appeared to be a relatively peaceful people, wearing only the hardware of their trade. They could be Mycenaean and that could mean another invasion. He would reveal the discovered stash when he returned to Knossos.

The blacksmith admired the quality and workmanship, which both exceeded his own skill. First, he inspected the daggers, finding two functional blades to replace his own, leaving his behind. Then it was on to the long swords, with blades nearly a foot longer than his. They were exquisite, but they weren't his sword; if he wanted another, he would forge it himself. The axes were too heavy and cumbersome to be practical.

The next opening was filled with small statuettes, pottery, and sealed vases. Some were obviously of religious significance. The vases were marked by their contents of the harvest.

The last side chamber had two different sizes of wooden barrels, numbering about four dozen, standing on end at the center of the room. Something caused a barrel to rock slightly, and Aiden drew his sword, pausing before it moved again. He cautiously approached and peeked over the top. There they were, his friends, all tied up.

"Oh, there you are, I wondered where you went," he humored as he removed their gags.

"Nice of you to join us," Hondo replied.

"I'm certainly not here to join you, although you look like you're having such a good time."

"It is great to see you or anybody for that matter, as long it's not the witch."

"Lilith, I'm sure."

"It was."

"What is it about you Egyptians that make you heed the call of strange women?"

"It must be a gift we have."

"Or a gift you don't. Did she have anything to say?"

"Lots of threats and promises, you know how women are. Things like, mind your own business and stay out of my way, don't test me, you know the drill."

"Sounds familiar. Is everybody okay?"

"Our egos are a little tarnished, but we'll recover."

"I don't think we should travel together, maybe it's a better idea to take separate ships to Egypt."

"We're not afraid of her, what's she going to do to us once we set sail?"

"That's what I worry about and you should too. The witch is capable of anything or everything. You could end up as a frog, a lizard, or something much worse."

Aiden walked his horse back to Knossos since he was the only one so equipped. It was decided, along the way, that Aiden would take the pharaoh's barge with Jib, and the rest would follow at a later sailing. Just before reaching the harbor, the blacksmith mounted his steed so they wouldn't arrive at the same time, with the eyes of Lilith upon them.

No one seemed to notice their entry back in the city, and there was no sign of an owl or raven lurking about. Even though they tried to keep a low profile, their number would give them away, so they avoided any gathering until the morning. The dawn brought them back together, surviving the night, and they headed to the docks.

There, atop one of the warehouses, was a blackbird perched on a weather vane. Aiden studied the bird for a moment, but it wasn't the witch. He scanned the harbor area, sure she must be present, and again, there was nothing unusual. Then when the two prepared to board, a sailor stepped up from behind the blacksmith, pressing against his back.

"I want my ring. Give it to me," he whispered in Aiden's ear.

The whisper startled him while tickling his ear at the same time, causing a slight twitch. He turned to face the sailor; his long hair flickered between gray and blonde while his lips a varied shade of red.

"Trade, it's the only way."

"Don't think for a moment your friends are safe."

"I leave without them, they have no part in this. The issue is between you and me."

"I'm not the one who got them involved."

"We only travel the same road, in safety, with different destinations. There's no benefit in their harm."

"The ring."

"The trade."

"You're becoming dangerously stubborn."

"And you continue to be unreasonable. We either both win or both lose. I can't see it any other way."

"See it my way and live."

"I have nothing more to deliberate. You've heard my terms, and they still stand. The sailor was a nice touch, though."

"You are a despicable excuse for a man."

"And you haven't fared any better as a witch, either. I'd say we started off on the wrong foot."

"Is everything okay?" Jib asked as the conversation had stretched out for several minutes.

"I think we're done, she was just leaving."

"She?"

"Lilith."

Jib had to give the sailor a second glance, trusting that Aiden knew what he was talking about. She didn't look that convincing as a sailor and appeared very agitated. He gave Aiden a hand, pulling him aboard the vessel, soon to depart, as the witch stood in defiance. Her stare alone could burn a hole through a man's soul.

"If you want to reconsider my proposal, you'll find me in Egypt. There's no need to shape-shift since I see you for who you are. Come to me in the flesh or don't come at all."

"Don't dictate to me, you're nothing but a blacksmith with limited skills, who can't admit he's already lost."

"So far, I've lost nothing, except my respect of one so powerful. You refuse to consider any reasonable solution to such a simple transaction. I'll see you in Egypt."

"Maybe sooner than you think, blacksmith, your confidence will be your downfall."

"Doubtful, but we'll play this game your way, for now."

The sailor walked off the docks to the shore, taking Lilith's form when he reached the sand. Not one person seemed to notice her transformation, odd, considering her physical attributes. It could be because they were under the influence of her spell. From there, she watched as the ship was untied from its berth, sails raised, and the voyage begun.

It was difficult for Jib to leave the others behind, even though it was for their own safety. Hondo would ensure they took the next transport out, hopefully without any interference from the witch.

None were aware that the wizard had interceded on their behalf, protecting those left behind. The temporary spell would shield them from Lilith's magic until they all arrived back home. The powers of Edric had reached their limit at such a distance, and if he had to cast another spell, he would need to cancel one.

The wizard's mirror would require his constant monitoring over the next two days. One mistake could jeopardize the entire quest, leaving them vulnerable to the will of the witch. Lilith was crafty and sadistic; if there was a loophole in Edric's magic, there was always a chance she could find it. Her intrusion could cause all his spells to collapse, leaving him unable to reinstate any protections at all.

He decided to try and keep the mirror focused on her. If his plan worked, he could study her every move and adjust his spells accordingly. The question was would she be able to trace his observations, through the mirror, back to him? Knowing the source of Aiden's protection could also backfire, negating the spells that guarded him.

The safeguards were tenuous at best. The quest had become a fragile game of the wizard's creative wit versus Lilith's dark powers. It was a test unlike any he'd experienced before. The queen of Haides had more influence and control than he, but his secrecy was the key to his success as long as he stayed one step ahead of her at all times.

Edric's thoughts were interrupted by a pounding at the door. He had no time for visitors, considering the situation at hand. Ariana was persistent in her knock, but he refused to answer. She continued for some time before finally giving up, easing the distraction to his ears and allowing him to concentrate on his actions.

Nefertiti's Gift

Aiden and Jib stood at the bow, peering out in the blue, where the water and sky seemed to blend in the middle. The blacksmith took the ruby necklace Edric had given him and held it out facing the sun. The red brilliance captivated the Egyptian who saw it for the first time. The blacksmith shared the purpose of the gift as the two followed the path of the radiant rays, some thirty feet out in the water.

"Strong, isn't it?"

"Very."

"I've seen it burn dried grass. I believe it can make water boil too if it was shallow enough."

"But can it find you a phoenix feather? That's the real question."

"Speaking of medallions, I'm supposed to give Meritaten's to the pharaoh, once I arrive at Amarna. Since you're still with me, I think you should deliver it."

"Not a chance in hell."

"But you're a member of the royal family."

"I'm only one of many nephews and the one who helped her escape. I don't think he wants to see me, at least, bringing him her necklace. She gave it to you, so you could get close to her father. Her method has purpose."

"Does that mean you won't travel with me to Amarna?"

"I'll go, but only to support your story and help win you favor with Akhenaten. Then I fade into obscurity, so I can make another escape to the island without interference."

"With help from the gods, Lilith, fate, or luck, it would be good to return together."

"I think luck is your best option, sorry to say, and mine is fate."

The ship sailed along the northern coast on its way to Mennefer, up the first tributary. Date palms began to appear on the western shore, and the farther they sailed up the Nile, the more prominent they became. Fruit hung from the stately trees, magnificently stunning in their stance with long green branches spread like fans in the sky. They were something new for the blacksmith to behold as he traveled through the oddities of the world. He'd never thought the lands could be so diverse or the characters so unique.

The ship reached the harbor of Mennefer, which the Greek's called Memphis, and berthed to unload its cargo. Due to the rise of Thebes, it was no longer the capital of Egypt. The port sat near the convergence of all the delta tributaries, and from here, Jib and Aiden would seek other transportation to Hermopolis, paying a toll to get there and another to pass beyond.

Mennefer was breathtaking. Palaces and temples rose up like a chain of mountains, dressed in shades of red, blue, and yellow. The city was the regional center of commercial trade with a high density of factories, workshops, and warehouses. It was considered the gateway to the kingdom and world trade, attracting a large number of foreigners, which made it the most populated city in the world.

From afar, three giant pyramids pierced the sky, each bigger than the other, built to honor previous pharaohs of the kingdom. They were so massive; it was difficult to accept man could erect such a structure. These stone monoliths were the ones sewn into Scota's rug.

Aiden was overcome by the size of everything around him. He was accustomed to living alone, outside two very small villages. The pace was too hectic, and the noise made it hard to concentrate. He could never stay very long in a place with such turbulent activity.

Pharaoh Akhenaten had a new temple under construction to honor Aten, his new deity of choice. It was his attempt to break the influence of the god Atum and the priests' power over the pharaoh. In addition, the capital was moved from Thebes to Amarna, where his new palace was being built. The changes were controversial among the people and unacceptable by the priesthood, breaking a long-standing tradition.

Aiden could see Scota in every woman. Their ankle-length tunics were tight fitting with revealing low necklines. The crimson and yellow linen was decorated with fringe trim, starch-pleated folds, and were suspended by straps over the shoulder. Jewelry was very diverse. Some had scarab rings, bracelets, and amulets or various combinations of each while others had pearl earrings, wide necklaces of gold, jasper, and turquoise or blue and green beads. The craftsmanship was unequaled, especially the detailed enamel work.

Most women wore black Nubian wigs of various cuts and eyes blackened by what Jib called kohl powder. They were fair-skinned and wore sandals, some decorated in jewels. Their beauty was astounding, and these were common people.

The men wore kilts of a heavier fabric, less jewelry, except for those who wore breastplates and donned black Nubian wigs or had shaved heads. They wore sandals too, but many wrapped their way up the shin. The blacksmith was most amazed at finding men with blackened eyes.

The unique dress and culture of the Egyptians was clearly impressive. There was a sense of equality among the people, each sharing their pride in the accomplishments of the dynasties and reflecting a sense of inner peace.

On their way toward the temple, Jib entered a small shop and purchased some kohl powder of his own. He stood before a wall mirror and applied the powder, smoothing the texture with his finger.

"Want some?"

"I don't think so. If I wore it, I'd look like I lost a fight."

"Maybe later, but Ariana would be pleased to receive such a gift."

"I'll consider it."

The products offered in the marketplace were similar to Knossos, except for the cultural differences, mainly focusing on women. Egypt had everything a female could possibly desire to enhance her beauty. Aiden knew he'd be remiss returning without gifts of such flattering attributes, not only for Ariana, but Princess Camille as well.

The toll boat was ready to head upriver, and the blacksmith was glad. He enjoyed Mennefer, but felt cramped by all the frenzied activity. They returned to the harbor and paid the toll. They would travel to meet with the pharaoh in Amarna before returning to Heliopolis on the delta.

Again, date palms dominated the western shore along with numbers of ibis among the reeds, all the way to Hermopolis. Many smaller boats navigated the waters carrying agricultural harvest in both directions while other vessels fished. The farther upriver, the more traffic they encountered.

According to Jib, the city was the center of science, mathematics, medicine, and astronomy. They believed that godlike beings came to earth and established Egypt, thus, worshiping the god Djhuty.

Hermopolis was also where the Emerald Tablet was buried in a secret chamber beneath a pyramid of Cheops. The rectangular green crystal plaque was written by the son of Adam, containing the sum of all knowledge and wisdom. The tablet challenged many Egyptian beliefs with the concept of one god but, at the same time, supported the theory of supernatural influence.

At a distance, the Djhuty Temple had a portico with double rows of pillars, six in each, forty feet high, painted with alternating yellow, red, and blue stripes. It was both grand in scale and architecture. They stayed the night in the city with only a short distance until reaching Amarna, which they found had been renamed Akhenaten by the pharaoh himself.

Today was a big day for the blacksmith. He was slightly nervous about the trip to Akhenaten and wanted to make his best impression when presented before the pharaoh. He was assured by Jib that when one called on the king, it was very formal in nature. Akhenaten would study Aiden's movements while determining the importance of his words. One or the other would need to stir interest or he would be dismissed. Of course, if he offered a gift, the pharaoh would be more tolerant.

Both dressed in their finest, with Jib clad in his native garb, looking like an Egyptian of status, which, of course, he was. Walking to the harbor, everyone acknowledged his presence, and Aiden realized it was the royal medallion he wore that required the recognition. Just being in Jib's company made the blacksmith feel important. They boarded a smaller vessel, being so close to the capital, without paying a toll, thanks to his family rank.

Approaching the newly built city, it was enclosed from behind by steep cliffs running north and south on the eastern bank. The capital appeared to be divided into three distinct sections with a crisp pristine appearance due to the newly whitewashed façade. Palaces and temples were faced with stone while less important buildings made of mud brick.

The first buildings they encountered were the northern palace, residence of the royal family, the palace of Queen Nefertiti, and a few homes of prosperous nature. The central city contained the Great Temple of Aten and the ceremonial Great Royal Palace, among others. To the south was mostly noble housing, all according to Jib. The western bank held a smaller palace of the pharaoh.

The harbor and docks covered both sides of the Nile with moored vessels of various kingdoms. The dress was diverse as were their status. The royal guards of the pharaoh were positioned at a variety of strategic locations, monitoring the movements and unloading of the foreign traders and diplomats.

The ceremonial palace wouldn't receive guests until the king was present. Jib considered taking the blacksmith to the royal residence, but decided to give him a short tour of the city instead. He wasn't prepared to arrive unannounced and wanted Aiden to experience the ceremonial appearance before the pharaoh.

They walked the incline, passing between the columns leading to the bridge spanning the road below. The bridge was supported by brick piers and had a covered causeway leading to the Great Royal Palace of formal residence. From the span, they could view the palace gardens; the massive Great Temple of Aten to the north; the smaller Aten temple, with its brick pillars, to the south; and the storehouses of grain. The road below was bustling with activity at the numerous shops, bakeries, and squares.

"Jibade, is that you?"

They both turned to greet the approaching voice of the royal sculptor.

"Thutmose."

"Where have you been? You know, your untimely disappearance created quite a stir with the royals."

"I'm sure, but it's a long story I'd rather not repeat over and over again. You'll hear the details soon enough. It looks like the pharaoh has kept you busy, new city and all."

"You have no idea, but things have settled down somewhat, although we still have construction going on. I'm working on sculptures of the royal family presently, if you'd like to come to workshop for a view."

"We might as well while we're waiting on the king."

They followed the sculptor to a large freestanding structure filled with stacks of uncut stone on both sides. The stone tables, at the back of the room, contained a number of unfinished pieces in various stages of completion. They entered the sculptor's private workshop at the back of the building where his royal images were lined along the entire length of a wooden table.

Jib and Aiden stood facing the row of sculpted busts. Most were projects needing more detail, but four were nearly complete.

"Aiden, I'd like you to meet Pharaoh Akhenaten."

The blacksmith was quick to notice the elongated skull and the rather feminine facial features of the sculpture, but said nothing.

"This one you know."

"Scota."

"Meritaten, the eldest daughter of pharaoh."

"Well, of course, force of habit."

"This is the young prince, Tutankhaten."

Aiden again notice the elongated skull, although not as predominate with his age. The last bust was the only one painted. It was beautifully crafted with a stunning female image.

"This striking bust is the Queen Nefertiti. It's flattering, Thutmose, but the queen is more dazzling in person."

"I agree."

"Well, Aiden, you've met what royals you can for now, the rest come later."

The three visited for a time, Thutmose exhibiting his skill with a chisel until it was time to pay a call on the pharaoh. Once more, Aiden was a little apprehensive. By the time they returned to the palace, there was already a line extending outside.

The long line held an array of bright colors, extending from the feet all the way to the elaborate headdresses. Mixed among the crowd was an assortment of weird-looking animals, instruments, and a touch of normal in the accompanying diplomats. Gifts, of various trades, were also abundantly apparent.

Jib escorted Aiden to the front of the line, creating some displeasure in the move. The blacksmith wasn't in a hurry to go next. He wanted to get a feel for the process first, so he took a place in line.

"Sire, the ambassador from Nubia."

With the announcement, Aiden watched the dark-skinned envoy step forward, stopping halfway to the throne and bowing before the king. The pharaoh, sitting next to his great royal wife with four daughters at her side and Tutankhaten at his, acknowledged the Nubian.

"Pharaoh, Nubia offers a creature fitting of your collection."

A servant stepped forward leading an ostrich. Aiden thought the long neck was rather odd, and the giant bird didn't look too happy either. The blacksmith considered how easy chickens were to raise, and they weren't aggressive either. Royalty was impressed, especially the prince.

"Does it fly?" the prince asked, with caution in his tone.

"No, but it can run like the wind."

"We are pleased," the pharaoh advised as the bird was led away.

Aiden asked Jib about the three formidable figures standing near the king.

"Ranefer, his general; Nakhtpaaten, chief minister; and Panehesy, the high priest of Aten."

"Pharaoh, the ambassador of Cyprus."

The envoy went forward with four attractive women, each rolling out colorful fabric, crisscrossing the marble floor and stopping at the base of the thrones.

"Queen Nefertiti, Cyprus brings you the latest fabric, new in color and design."

"I too am pleased."

Her handmaidens stepped forward to receive the gifts, stopping at the throne of the queen, so she and her daughters could feel the material. Aiden was next, and he had to repeat his introduction, three times, before he was understood. Jib found the effort to announce him amusing.

"Aiden, the blacksmith from the Celt Isle."

He moved forward with confidence, and every eye in the palace was on him. His announcement created a stir of curiosity and doubt among those in the room and a perplexed look on the face of the king and queen.

"Pharaoh, I greet you on behalf of my island, but moreover, I stand before you as a messenger of Meritaten."

There was awe and eerie quiet that consumed the room as the king and queen looked at each other in disbelief.

"Meritaten?"

"Sire, if I may approach the throne?"

"Please step forward," Nefertiti spoke with some excitement in her voice.

Aiden moved closer, taking the princess's medallion from around his neck, attempting to give the necklace to the pharaoh, who deferred to his queen.
"I bring you love and good health with her best regards."
The monarchs eyed the medallion as Princess Ankhesenpaaten eased forward.
"Where is my sister?"
"She lives on the coast of my island."
"And why is it you bear this medallion from such a distance?" the pharaoh asked.
"I was sent here by the princess to fulfill my quest of the phoenix feather and to carry her words."
"Did you travel all this way alone?"
Before Aiden could answer, Jib stepped up from behind.
"No, my king, he did not."
"Jibade, I hope you can explain."
The king waved both men to the throne, looking frustrated and confused.

"We will talk of this once these ceremonies are complete. Jibade, take our young blacksmith to the north palace and wait for us."
The two acknowledged the monarch and were led by the high priest down a corridor behind the throne room. Once outside, they were joined by the queen's handmaidens, all the children, and the king's guard, who escorted the large party to the palace of the queen.
The exterior of the complex had an extensive garden court enclosure, facing the river and several animal pens to the rear. They walked past several rooms, all with garden-view windows, on their way to the central chamber, which was painted in a continuous mural of natural life in the marshes.
While the children looked on Aiden as an unusual guest, the elder daughters were curious enough to approach him with questions. Meketaten, twelve, and Ankhesenpaaten,

eleven, both appeared older than their years, already being groomed by the family as potential rulers of the kingdom and skilled in the aesthetics of makeup. They were satisfied with his answers, although some queries required a response from Jib.

The younger siblings, ranging in age from two to seven, soon ignored the presence of the blacksmith in the family chamber. They played with dolls, many in the image of the gods, and chased each other around the room. Setepenre, the youngest, broke into tears at times, feeling exclusion and struggling to keep up.

Several hours passed before the king and queen finally emerged. They seated themselves, one on each side of their guests, while Nefertiti's maidens supplied refreshments and began filling the chamber's large table with an abundance of food.

"Jibade, I can't begin to tell you how disappointed I am with your actions in this matter. It is unacceptable that you aided Meritaten's flee from the kingdom. Can you explain before I decide on your fate?"

"Sire, one can't change her mind once she has made the decision. She is a princess, and I am but a cousin. She feared for her life, and I was obligated to obey her commands. Meritaten would have left with or without my help, and I couldn't protect her if I stayed behind."

"Why would she fear for her life?"

"She dreamt of a great plague that would sweep across the kingdom and the impact of the religious changes threatening the country's stability."

"There has been no plague."

"Not yet, but it's coming."

"Why did you not tell us of her plans?" the queen asked.

"Because I was sworn to secrecy, and she knew you'd never let her leave."

The entire family moved to the banquet table, with the pharaoh placing Aiden and Jibade at his sides.

"Did you not fear my reprisal at your return?"

"I did, but the truth, sire, it was never intended I return to Egypt."

Jib shared the purpose of his involvement and the exploits of the quest, which ultimately resulted in his assurance the message from the princess reached the family safely, through Aiden, regardless of any retribution he surely would face.

"Blacksmith, we're grateful you befriended our daughter, carrying her medallion and message of life. We were consumed by her death and you bring peace to our hearts," the queen spoke.

"It has been my privilege and respect of a friend."

"Tell me of your quest for the feather of the phoenix."

Aiden shared his story, love of the princess, conflicts with Lilith and creatures of the dark side, and his purpose for seeking the Temple of Heliopolis. The sincerity of his heart and the dedication to the quest were evident in his tale.

"How long are you willing to commit to this quest?"

"As long as I live and breathe, nothing else matters."

"Such dedication is admirable, but capturing a feather of a firebird that only returns to the temple every five hundred years is unrealistic, even if your search is within its cycle."

"I have to believe I can accomplish the task and I will, one way or another."

The pharaoh considered all that was shared in their meeting, stepping away from the table for a conference with the queen before making his decree.

"Jibade, I could take your life, without remorse, for what you've done, but instead, we have decided you take Aiden to Heliopolis. I will have a ship waiting in the harbor with a crew from my guard. You will sail back to this island and bring back our daughter. She will return. Is this understood? Failure to do so will cost your life, and you will never see Egypt again."

"Sire, I'm grateful for your mercy. I will do my best."

"For your sake, I hope your best is good enough."

Aiden and Jib stayed the night in the queen's palace while the family retreated to the great royal palace, farther to the north. Akhenaten and the young prince returned in the early morning with his chariot. He drove the blacksmith around his dream city, including the tour of his zoo.

The pharaoh took extreme pleasure in his collection of animals, separated by walls and cages, among the canopy of the gardens. The strangeness of their kind was like a spell had been cast upon them. While some were docile, others would surely consume a man with little effort. Aiden could appreciate the bizarre oddities, but wondered why one would amass such a collection, keeping his thoughts to himself.

The prince, with his braided Horus lock, maintained a dignified image throughout the tour until they arrived at the bakery. There was something about the aroma of bread infused with dates and raisins, which excited him beyond his noble place. The hot bread and pastries coated in butter tantalized their taste buds while bringing the tour to a climax.

The three rode the chariot to the great royal palace where the queen and five princesses awaited their arrival. The queen had the blacksmith follow her to the royal treasure chamber, which was filled with riches from around the world. The amassed collection was a bounty of wealth and affluence.

Nefertiti, drawn to a corner table with a marble top and golden legs, grasped one piece, gifting the blacksmith a golden amulet on a golden chain. The amulet bore the insignia of the pharaoh, and the queen put it around his neck.

"This will aid in your travels while in Egypt and abroad. May Aten guide your journey home."

"Thank you, Your Highness. My journey home is but a dream at present."

"You are closer than you think to reaching your goal. I believe Meritaten knew that when she sent you to me, although she couldn't be sure how I would respond. I have something that may help with your quest."

Nefertiti walked to another table, which among other treasures, held a carved green soapstone chest. She retrieved the box and returned with it cradled in her arms.

"This chest holds a treasure that's been passed down from one pharaoh to the next for over a thousand years. It is not mine to give, but if I entrust it to your safekeeping, you can take it to my daughter as a symbol of devotion. The one catch, either the princess or you, as a prince, must return the gift to its rightful home."

"I'm willing to commit to such an agreement."

"I had confidence that you would."

The queen rested the chest in the blacksmith's arms and removed the lid. Aiden was speechless, his facial expression frozen in time. A phoenix feather lay right before his very eyes. He was so overcome, tears rolled down his cheek.

"This green box holds my dreams, and I'm grateful you deem me worthy of your trust."

"You've already proved your worth upon your arrival. Guard it with your life and ensure its return."

"I can't carry the feather in this chest without creating curiosity of the contents. There must be something smaller?"

"Thutmose is making a narrow metal sleeve, so the feather can't be damaged. He should be here shortly."

"I saw your image on the painted bust in his workshop. It's beautiful, but it doesn't do you justice."

"Aiden, there's no need for you to flatter me now. I've already granted your wish."

"Beauty is in the eyes of the beholder and your beauty runs deeper than anyone can see."

"Thank you, young blacksmith, future prince, and someday king."

"Thank you for all you've done, Your Highness, I'm forever indebted and shall never forget your favor."

Thutmose entered the treasure room, carrying his specially designed carrier. He carefully slipped the feather into the crafted silver case and handed it to Aiden after the queen had retrieved the soapstone chest from his arms. They returned to the royal chamber, rejoining the family. The children were sitting on the floor, surrounding the pharaoh as he was sharing a story. He urged the children to entertain themselves for a time, inviting Jib and Aiden to walk outside.

"There's no longer a need to make the journey to Heliopolis as you know, so my barge is ready to carry you to Mennefer.

The king's guard will be waiting with a ship that will take you home. There are now two things that must be returned to me, the feather and my daughter. Aten travels with you."

Both men were grateful and promised compliance with the pharaoh's decree. The blacksmith, eager to get started and ready to claim his rite, wasted no time heading to the docks.

Two Feathers

Once onboard the pharaoh's barge, they settled back and relaxed. The barge was decorated with bright pennants and colorful fabric panels, which served as dividers as well as sunscreens. The boat was built for comfort, not speed, so their sail to Mennefer would take much longer. They weren't alone with the guard, several servants, and dancers also aboard. The two men were treated like pharaohs, making the trip gratifying and entertaining.

Aiden reclined back on a soft cushion and closed his eyes, grasping the white hanky of his beloved. All he could think about was Ariana. He couldn't wait to see the look on her face once she saw the feather was in hand. Thoughts of taking her in his arms for that first kiss, the wedding, and wedding bed, all crossed his mind. All he had to do was be the first to return and claim his victory. It wasn't likely anyone else could find a feather as fast as he, if there was one. All he had to do was take care of the feather he had. He couldn't have been more satisfied.

"That's a broad smile you're wearing. What are you thinking about?" the Egyptian asked.

"Ariana and home. What are you thinking?"

"Hondo and where he's at."

"I was surprised they didn't show up at the palace."

"You know, we weren't very clear about where we were going first. They may have gone to Heliopolis."

"Do we wait for them before we sail?"

"No, we can't. I'm not too worried, though, they'll find their own way back."

Once they arrived in Mennefer, the pharaoh had a seagoing vessel waiting. While the ship was being loaded with supplies, Jib took the blacksmith to view the pyramids in Giza, a short distance away. The two rode to the complex on the backs of camels after the Egyptian convinced Aiden the spirited and sometimes stubborn animal was safe to mount. It was an awkward ride for one used to a horse, and horses didn't spit.

The pyramids dominated the skyline, but the detail of the site wasn't revealed until they'd reached the Great Sphinx. There were as many temples as there were pyramids and a long causeway leading to the second largest. The panoramic view was very impressive, both in size and architectural achievement.

"The great pyramid was built by Pharaoh Khufu. The second by his son, Pharaoh Khafre, and the smallest was constructed by his grandson Pharaoh Menkaure. All three contain their burial chambers. The three smaller pyramids to the left are those of queens," Jib explained.

"Magnificent! How could they build something so massive?"

"With contributions by the gods of the sun, the stars, and a multitude of slaves."

"The gods must have had an enormous impact to complete such a feat."

"One can't underestimate their power and influence, that's why they're gods."

"And what is this creature before us?"

"The Great Sphinx with the body of a lion and head of Pharaoh Khafre. The image is his rendition. Traditionally, a sphinx has the body of a lion, wings of a grand bird, with the breast and face of a woman. She is said to eat those who can't answer her riddle."

"And the riddle?"

"What creature walks on four legs in the morning, two in the afternoon, and three in the evening?"

"Can you answer the riddle?"

"A man. As a baby he crawls, an adult he stands upright, and with old age comes a cane."

"With the women I've encountered so far, it might be important I know the answer."

"Knowledge is power in the right hands."

They rode back to the harbor with the blacksmith still adjusting to his camel. The beast seemed to sense its return to food and water, moving at a quickened pace. Upon their arrival, they were astounded to find Hondo and Dak waiting for their return. After a warm greeting, they boarded ship for the return to Crete.

"How did you know where to find us?" Jib asked.

"It seems to be common knowledge. Everyone's talking about the pharaoh's ship sailing to the Celt Isle. By the description, we knew it was you," Hondo answered.

"What happened to Horus and Doncor?"

"They both decided to remain in Egypt, so from here on, it's only the four of us."

"That's not unexpected. I thought someone would stay behind. This is home after all."

"If the word is out, my competition may also be aware. Hopefully, that doesn't create any complications along the way."

"You could be right, Aiden."

It was almost dark by the time they reached the mouth of the delta. A celebration of sorts took place once the ship hit the open sea and its sails were full. For the first time in their journey, they were on the way home. It was a good feeling as they watched the Egyptian coast slowly disappear.

Early on the third day from their departure, Dak called his comrades to the bow and pointed to an approaching vessel. The ship was the Argo, crossing their course, headed southwest toward the northern coast of the continent. They thought it was odd to be headed in such a direction, but it was the Argo and who knew what adventure they were on now.

It was still daylight when the ship reached the Minoan harbor. The captain found a berth and tied up to the dock.

Some supplies would need unloading and others stored, so the night in the city was theirs, including the guard. They stood outside the inn, drinking their beverage of choice, when an arrow whizzed past Aiden's head, embedding in a wooden lamppost inches from his face.

Everyone dropped into a crouch, searching the area around them. Everything appeared normal as residents walked the street among four carts. No strangers in the darkness or any drawn bow were found. To get a better look, weapons were drawn, and they fanned out from the post. Finding no assassin, they returned to the inn. Aiden cut the arrow out of the post and they all went inside.

"Think it was Tobias?" Jib asked the blacksmith.

"Who else could it be?"

"Then he must know."

Jib convinced the guard to conduct a wider search, and Aiden provided the description. About two hours later, one of the guards asked them to step outside for identification. Tobias stood in the arms of the guard, not surprised by Aiden's approach.

"That's him alright. Where are your manservant's?"

"Yes, it's me, blacksmith. My servants are dead, now turn me loose."

"Sure, so you can try and kill me again since you have no one to carry out your dirty work."

"I don't know what you're talking about."

"This," he said, pulling the arrow from his quiver. "You're not as good a shot as I thought you were."

"That's not mine."

Aiden reached across and pulled an arrow from Tobias's quiver to compare the two, but they didn't match.

"I told you it's not mine, now let me go."

"Just because they don't match doesn't prove your innocence. You could have picked up this arrow anywhere."

"I could have, but I didn't, although with you out of my way, the loss wouldn't be great. Release me now or deal with me later."

"There is no later. You're staying with us so I can keep an eye on you all the way home. You won't get a second chance, Tobias."

"You'll answer for this."

"To whom, there's no one here to listen. Behave yourself, and we won't throw you overboard on the way back."

The guard took the suspected assassin back to the ship and locked him in the hold while the rest enjoyed the evening. Aiden's luck was still intact though his confidence was tested. The blacksmith wondered if Tobias knew he had the feather. It didn't seem too likely; otherwise, he'd have caught Aiden alone. Now he wouldn't concern himself with Tobias for the remainder of his successful quest.

In the morning after they'd set sail, Tobias was released and given the freedom to walk the decks. He approached the blacksmith without hesitation, despite his colleagues standing nearby. As he drew closer to Aiden, so did they.

"You're not home yet, blacksmith, so don't get too comfortable. Again you have offended me, and it's my right to challenge. I won't do it here, but expect it once we reach the castle. You will die by my sword, and when you do, the feather will mean nothing."

"What makes you think I have a feather?"

"You wouldn't be going back without one, but it doesn't matter. You'll never marry the princess."

"She will be my wife and you'll be there to witness, now go bother someone else with your petty threats."

Tobias did back away with a look of despise. He spent the next several days sitting on a barrel, carving a piece of wood with his dagger. He whittled the stick like he was taking slices out of Aiden's hide and made sure he sat where the blacksmith could see him. He was obviously pissed, getting caught in his dishonorable behavior, and Aiden did his best to pay him no mind. The blacksmith focused on making a necklace from the bear's teeth and claws.

The ship would arrive at the Balearic Islands in seven days. The port would be their last stop on the long journey home.

It would be good to arrive, but even better to leave. Passing through the channel at the Pillars of Hercules would leave the inland sea behind them.

Edric's mirror showed the wizard that Aiden was on his way home with the feather. He thought about telling the princess, but decided to wait. He wanted to keep Aiden's surprise for him to reveal. The blacksmith was still a long way from home and anything could happen. Soon, the ship would be close enough for the wizard to see any future events in the cauldron and then he'd feel more comfortable.

Word had reached the castle of a battle between Scota's Egyptians and the Nordics at the northern shores of the island. They were able to repel the attack in the defense of an established settlement, but the victory had cost the princess dearly. She lost her husband Theo. The wizard was so occupied with Aiden's travels; he hadn't viewed the cauldron for some time, or he would have been able to foretell the event. There was nothing in his power that could have prevented the outcome, with his spells at their limit, but he felt the burden nonetheless.

The Egyptian ship entered the Balearic harbor, reaching the halfway point of the voyage. This stop would be more pleasant than Aiden's last, having been shanghaied. Tobias's detestable plan hadn't worked out the way he'd expected, the blacksmith was sure of that. There was some discussion on whether they should let him go ashore or not, but they decided to keep him under surveillance rather than enslaved.

"You're free to leave the ship, Tobias. It's your choice whether you get back on board. If it was up to me, I'd leave you here, it's no less than you deserve," Aiden advised.

"You and I have a destiny to fulfill. We sail together, unless you're man enough to face me here."

"Don't be in such a rush to meet your maker. We have plenty of time to settle this."

"When we do, I'll be the one placing the coin in your mouth for the ferryman."

"Think what you like."

The port had a very relaxed atmosphere, which was good for everyone, even though they wouldn't stay long. They were back at sea in a few hours, sailing for the Iberian coast. It would take three more days to reach the Pillars of Hercules, so-called after the hero had narrowed the channel to keep sea monsters at bay.

Phoenicians considered the waters beyond the end of the known world. Anyone who didn't heed the warnings would surely be eaten alive or go down with their ship. Those crazy enough to test the limits of the turbulent water would crash over the edge, never to be heard from again. Facing one sea monster was more than enough for this quest, so nobody wanted to challenge the theory. The captain didn't care whether the story was true or not, his ship would hug the coast, and keeping the mainland in view was suitable to all.

Smoke rose from several settlements as they sailed along the mainland. They were variable in size and origin, but none appeared to have a port. The eastern shore of the peninsula had some Egyptian colonies, according to Jib, but none had settled the western coast as far as he knew.

Tobias continued to whittle away on his piece of wood, with no detail or design in his carving. He appeared less aggressive in his manner for now, but that was likely to change.

Aiden still focused his thoughts on the princess and wondered what might be going through her mind as she waited for a husband. As each day passed, she faced the possibility of a suitor less worthy and unloved. The prolonged wait had to be frustrating for Ariana, not knowing her fate.

The ship neared the pale-gray pillars of the channel the following day. The limestone monoliths rose dramatically, over a thousand feet high, with the sheer rock cliff, off the starboard, the more impressive of the two. As they slowly traversed through the strait, the face of the two immense rocks exposed dozens of caves at various levels, carved out of their limestone walls.

To Aiden's amazement, Lilith sat on the lip of a cave opening, halfway up the starboard side in full view of everyone on the vessel. She made no attempt to hide her identity, making sure everyone received her message.

"I want my ring back!"

Her powerful statement echoed between the two cliffs, gripping all attention in her direction. She was persistent; the blacksmith had to give her that. He considered giving back the ring since he had the feather in his possession, but her refusal to be reasonable in their past encounters changed his mind. He wasn't home yet, and the ring might still serve a purpose.

"My ring or my wrath!"

They navigated the channel, leaving the witch with her own echoes. Aiden wondered if Lilith planned to follow him to the island or even the castle. She wasn't done with him yet, that was evident, and the voyage was getting shorter. He would be expecting her to make another appearance.

A herald knocked on the door of the wizard with a summons by the king. It was the middle of a hot afternoon when he arrived at the castle and was led to the queen's garden courtyard. There, the royal family was gathered for Edric's disclosure. The monarchs had maintained the garden since the queen's death, even adding a white gazebo where the princesses relaxed in the shade. The wizard sat at the white wooden table between the king and the prince as the girls came to join in the greetings.

"I love the roses this time of year, fragrant and colorful. It makes me want a garden of my own," the wizard shared.

"We all know you're too busy for a garden, Edric, but you're welcome to enjoy ours at your leisure," the king assured.

They all chatted briefly, over hard cider, about the Nordic attack on the Egyptians before the topic returned to the purpose of the invitation.

"What of the quest? You know that's why you're here," Darian asked.

"I can tell you this, three who declared, have begun their return to the castle. One has the feather in his possession."

"Is Aiden among the three?" Ariana begged for an answer.

"He is, princess, I'm glad to say."

The king could see her sincere excitement by the radiant glow on her face. She'd already made her choice and would have no other, which her father strongly approved.

"Which three return?" the king asked.

"Aiden, Tobias, and a Nordic."

"And who has the feather?"

"That, I can't say, sire, it could be any of the three."

"How can you be so glad for me, Edric, if you can't say? You know more than you reveal," Ariana challenged his answer.

The wizard wanted to tell the truth, but the truth would deny Aiden his right to proclaim triumph in his conquest before the throne. He couldn't take that away from him.

"Princess, I'm glad Aiden returns alive whether he has the feather or not."

"How do either of us benefit if he arrives without one? Tell me what remains unsaid and tell me now."

Edric paused, knowing he had to comply with her request. His answer had to satisfy the question or she would persist.

"Wizard," the king prompted an answer without any further delay.

"There is more than one feather among the three. It depends on who gets here first."

It wasn't the answer Ariana wanted to hear, but it was enough to get the wizard off the hook. She assumed the blacksmith had a feather, and the quest had become a race.

"Who is closer of the three?" the king inquired.

"Distance is questionable, but the three could reach the island on the same day."

"I would never have expected the quest to end in such a way."

"Nor I."

"Ariana, you're set on the blacksmith, I know, but you need to prepare yourself for the possibility of another. I made this decree and I can't change the outcome. Whatever happens, you will accept the one I declare, regardless of your heart. Is that understood?"

"Yes, Father, I will honor your word, but I don't have to like. If my husband is not Aiden, it won't be a marriage and I shan't ever be happy."

The wizard finished his cider, with none asking about his green beard. Ariana followed his departure through the castle, stopping him in the great hall.

"Is all you said truth, Edric?"

"I've nothing to gain through a lie."

"Sorry, I didn't mean to sound disrespectful. My heart is heavy and I thought, maybe, there was something more that would lift my spirit."

"Nothing more, my lady. Aiden is subject to his own destiny, whatever that might be. I've helped him as much as I could, but now it's up to him finish the quest and I can't interfere."

"Thank you for all you've provided my love, may we both pray it wasn't in vain."

After days of tedious travel, the Egyptian ship finally entered the Celtic channel with another day's sail to its narrowest gap. The island never looked so good to the blacksmith and thoughts of his princess lingered. He closed his eyes and visualized her beautiful eyes and full lips, framed by her golden strands. Another day felt like an eternity.

News of the approaching Egyptian ship reached the king. He sent out his heralds with a decree that all should assemble in the courtyard the following day to celebrate the betrothal of the princess and a hero's return. He wanted the event to be a spectacle that all would remember.

The ship dropped anchor before reaching Scota's settlement where the shortest distance to the castle followed along the lower road. The final leg of Aiden's journey would be on foot. The launch was lowered for Aiden, Tobias, and two Egyptian guards, but before the guard could board the small vessel, Tobias drew his dagger.

From behind, he held it to the blacksmith's throat and forced him to sit and man the oars. He had Aiden row the launch away from the ship with the point of his blade pressed against his skin. The pressure of the dagger was enough to draw blood.

Once Tobias was comfortable with the separation, he had the blacksmith stop.

"I'll take that feather now and deal with you later, once I'm prince."

"You'll never be prince."

"We'll see about that. Give me the feather."

Aiden handed the feather over to Tobias, was hit on the head with the butt of his dagger and pushed overboard. As the blacksmith tread water, several arrows were launched from the ship, some stuck in the launch, others pierced the water, but none hit the target. Jib dove into the cold water and swam to the blacksmith, pulling him back to the ship. Tobias had beached the launch before they were back on board.

"I don't know how we could have let that happen," Jib apologized to his friend.

"I'm okay, not to worry."

"But he's got the feather."

"A peacock feather."

"What?"

"I thought I needed something to ensure the safekeeping of the phoenix feather, so I bought the peacock in Crete."

"That was smart. So Tobias is headed to the castle with a fake."

"He is and doesn't know it."

"What are you going to do now?"

"Swim to the beach."

"Then I'm going with you. I'm already wet and don't want to miss the look on Tobias's face when he finds out his feather is fake."

Both men dove off the ship, pulling a rope they would tie to the longboat. Once they reached the sandy shore, the launch was secured, and the crew drew it back to the boat. They pulled up anchor and headed farther north to the Egyptian settlement.

The two friends began their trek to the castle as their wet clothes slowly began to dry. Their hour's walk cut through the heavy canopy of the forest where something lay in the road ahead. They approached the heap to discover it was Tobias with an arrow in his back and no feather.

"I didn't expect to see the look on his face so soon," Jib admitted.

"Me either, but look at this arrow, it matches the one in my quiver. It wasn't Tobias who tried to take my life, and he probably wasn't responsible for my shanghai either."

"Who then?"

"I don't know, but we'll find his murderer when we reach the castle."

The gathering in the courtyard waited to receive their champion with the royal family seated at the portico. Ariana had never felt so apprehensive in her life, and the anticipation was building for everyone but her. While everyone was focused on the castle's open gates, she refused, fearing the first face she saw would not be the one she loved.

She involved herself in a meaningless conversation with Camille when she spotted the wizard and waved him forward. Edric followed her direction hesitantly, knowing her purpose of the summons.

"Tell me he's close."

"He is, but so is another and one no longer contends."

"I can't stand this waiting and not knowing. Won't you tell me more?"

"No, my lady, there's nothing left to tell, you must believe in your heart."

"I try, but fear my heart will be broken beyond repair."

Then the announcement was made of a man approaching the gates. The princess suddenly felt sick to her stomach. The king gave her a quick look as she buried her head in her hands. Camille tried to comfort her sister, but instead was the one to give her the bad news.

"It's not him!"

Ariana wouldn't raise her head as tears filled her eyes. It was the worst that could happen, and she didn't know how she could ever get through the heartbreaking moment, then she felt her father's reassuring hand on her back.

"Ariana, you are a princess and must present yourself so. Swallow your disappointment and honor your father. One day, you will be queen and better understand the complexities of rank as did your mother."

Wiping her eyes, the princess slowly raised her head, giving her father a strained smile. She looked upon the blond Nordic, her future prince, and felt like she couldn't breathe. He gave her a nod, which she grudgingly returned.

"Sire, my name is Sven. I bring you the phoenix feather in exchange for the honor of your daughter's hand."

"Step forward, young Nordic. Bring me this feather that seals your fate."

He stepped forward and laid his prize in the king's hand, bowing before him. The king stood as he motioned the Nordic to his feet.

"I hereby proclaim the quest absolute. Sven has triumphed for the hand of Princess Ariana and the adoration of the people. I decree a royal wedding, one week hence."

Ariana's heart sank as her future prince was invited to join the royal family under the portico. She gripped her hands in a fist as they lay at her side, fearing he would approach for a kiss. The thought turned her stomach, having saved her kiss for only one man. Now the Nordic stood before her holding out his hands to lift the princess to her feet. She suddenly felt faint as she began to rise.

"Sire, you have been tricked by a fraud, liar, and murderer!" Aiden shouted as he passed through the gates with Jib at his side.

Sven let go of Ariana's hands and drew his sword as the princess fell back in her chair. He was quickly met by the king's guard and disarmed. Taking a deep breath, Ariana peeked around the Nordic to see her blacksmith challenging her father's decree. If there was satisfaction, it would surely come now. Her love had arrived just in time to save her from this nightmare and claim her heart.

"Aiden, can you prove your accusations?"

"I can, sire, if you would allow me."

"Step forward."

"The feather you hold in your hand is that of a peacock. I bought it in Crete as a diversion. This day, Tobias stole the feather from me and was murdered by the Nordic in the forest along the low road to the coast."

"He lies!"

"Silence or I'll have you gagged. Aiden, can you prove this to be the same feather?"

"If you look at the tip, sire, you'll see I dipped it in black ink."

The king examined the tip, and it was as the blacksmith described.

"Take this impostor to the dungeon and hold him for the gallows."

The Nordic tried to escape, but was quickly subdued and dragged away from the courtyard by the guards.

"So, Aiden, you've rebuffed his claim. Please tell me you possess the true feather."

"Sire, I do. The feather was given to me by Pharaoh Akhenaten and Queen Nefertiti of Egypt with the condition it must be returned."

"Can you prove your claim? I've already been deceived once today."

"Sire, if I may speak on Aiden's behalf?" Jib interjected.

"You may if you can substantiate his contention."

"My name is Jibade, nephew to the queen. I was present when she entrusted the phoenix feather to Aiden's capable hands. She did so with gratitude of his heroic accomplishments and compassionate commitment to the Egyptian royal family. He is your rightful prince."

"Can I see this elusive feather?"

Aiden was proud to step forward, handing the king his silver case.

"Sire, the face of the container is stamped with the pharaoh's royal seal."

"Impressive. You've thought of everything."

The princess was surprisingly calm while Aiden proved his claim. The wizard was right about believing in her heart.

Aiden was her man, and he'd proven his worth in every way possible. She was so proud of him. Her father took her hand and gave her the biggest smile she'd ever seen. He, too, was pleased with the final outcome of the quest.

"I hereby proudly decree, Aiden has proven his claim without question or challenge. His merit is beyond reproach. His deeds unsurpassed. He has won the hand of the princess and the respect of the kingdom in every way. Their wedding shall be one week hence."

King Darian and Princess Ariana left the shade of the portico and approached the future prince, putting her hand in his. Their eyes met in an intently passionate gaze of devotion, and their first embrace sealed their fate as lovers. Dreams do come true.

"You're all wet."

"It's the price I paid to be prince."

"Your clothes aren't those of a prince."

"No, princess, I am but a pauper."

"I must get you out of these clothes as soon as possible."

"You'll have to be patient for a week to do that."

"Kiss me, blacksmith, before I change my mind."

Their first kiss was everything they both had imagined. The wait was over, except for their wedding, and love did conquer all, including the kingdom. They returned to the portico, hand and hand, the king relinquishing his seat to the blacksmith. The two enjoyed the celebration between their longing gazes.

The following week flew by like the wind. Aiden visited the wizard to thank him for all he'd done. Without his help, the blacksmith never would have succeeded. Edric revealed his mirror, the cauldron, and the impact of the various spells he'd cast. He was truly the wizard of wizards.

He heard the fate of Theo and the Nordic attack, knowing they were the same Nordic pirates he had encountered crossing the channel. He was sad for Scota and missed her warm smile. He visited her old settlement on his first ride with the princess, sharing the tales of his journey along the way and how Scota and Edric had aided his cause. They gave their condolences to Jib and the Egyptians who would stay while they searched for their princess. A funeral wreath was tossed in the water and carried away by the current.

The day before the wedding, Aiden went to the castle to deliver his gifts to the princesses. It was a strange feeling not needing an announcement or an escort to visit. He found Ariana and Camille sitting together in the gazebo, having a hilarious conversation, which subsided on his approach.

"Ladies, don't stop on my account."

"It's on your account we're laughing," Camille revealed.

"That doesn't sound good."

"Oh, it's all good, my wonderful prince. We're only having girl talk. It wouldn't interest you," Ariana consoled.

"I brought you both gifts from Egypt. Fragrances and oils used by their women and the queen herself, said to charm a man, and enhance a woman's beauty, but I see you're both too lovely to need such enhancements. Please forgive me."

"A woman can never be too beautiful for the man she loves. She wants his eyes to see only her, but before I forgive you, tell me of these women who charm you."

"They sit before me, my princess."

"Does this flattery work with all women?"

"Only when I come bearing gifts."

"Then you are surely forgiven. Let's see this magic you bring these lowly princesses."

No sooner had Aiden presented his gift, they leapt to their feet and ran back into the castle, leaving him to ponder his reward. As he prepared to leave, a handmaiden arrived. She bowed while resting a pile of folded clothes and new pair of boots at his feet, then scurried away.

As he was departing the garden, Gideon happened by and Aiden gave the prince his gift of a sling from the Balearic's. The prince was pleased to be receiving a brother and was more than pleased with his sister's choice in men. The blacksmith found his way out, somewhat impatient, knowing he had to wait even one more day.

It was wedding day. Aiden traveled to the gatehouse at Edric's request to prepare for the event of his life. He thought he'd be nervous, but was totally composed, which is more than he could say of the wizard. His hair was white, for the sanctity of marriage, and his cloak the color of red, for the purity of heart. The blacksmith, dressed in his new clothes, looked every bit a prince and handsome as well. He would surely please his lady.

Together, they walked through the gathering crowd, entering the castle on their way to the chapel. The room was lit with a thousand candles and a selected number of guests. He took his place at the altar and waited with the priest for the royal family to arrive. He'd dreamed of this day for what seemed an eternity, and now, time stood still.

Finally, Prince Gideon entered the chapel and took his place at Aiden's side, giving him a subtle bump with his shoulder and a smile of approval. Aiden handed him the light-pink amethyst wedding ring he had set in Crete.

"If she wasn't my sister, I'd marry her myself. She is stunning."

Before Aiden could reply, Camille made her entry, tossing white daisies from her basket. She looked older than her years, every bit a woman in her Egyptian makeup. She winked at the groom-to-be, as she passed, taking her place opposite him.

Now Aiden became overwhelmed with anticipation, closing his eyes for a moment, giving thanks in silence to all who made his dream possible. He was grateful to have such a long list to thank, an indebtedness he would one day repay.

There was an awe that filled the room when the king and the future bride entered. She was almost too beautiful for Aiden to look at, a vision of an angel in her long white gown. Again, they couldn't take their eyes off each other as she paced to meet him. Her radiant glow was enough to light the room, and she took his hands in hers.

"You are so beautiful, Ariana, but your smell precedes you," he said with a smile.

"You look very handsome too, Aiden, and I smell good, but you'll have to wait to appreciate the hypnotic power of my essence. Can you do that?"

"I'm already under your spell, princess, and my dream of waiting is over."

"Then let's live our dreams together and consecrate this union for the ages, shall we?"

"I've never been more ready to fulfill your expectations than I am this very moment and the rest of our lives."

"I love you, Aiden."

"I love you more, Ariana."

"If you two would stop talking and performing your own vows, we might be able to get this ceremony started," the king urged, with a little impatience.

The comment brought a giggle that swept through the chapel; even the king became vulnerable to his own urging, and it took a few moments to regain the sanctity of the ceremony so they could continue. The glorious wedding resumed without any further interruptions before culminating in their "I do's."

The ring on her finger was perfect. The color was dazzling as was she. Its beauty and hers made a statement that none could deny.

The elated couple shared a passionate kiss to seal their vows. The blessed event would bring new life to the kingdom and begin an era of hope and prosperity for all. When they exited the castle and entered the square hand in hand, they received an unprecedented and jubilant roar. The newlyweds had become the prince and princess of the people.

Character Map

Celtic Island

Aiden = Blacksmith, future prince
Ariana = Princess
Darian = King
Gideon = Prince
Camille = Princess
Edric = Wizard
Tobias = King's guard
Scota = Meritaten, Egyptian princess
Theo = Gaytheios, Egyptian prince
Jib = Jibade, Egyptian escort
Hondo = Egyptian escort
Dak = Dakarai, Egyptian escort
Atum = Egyptian escort
Don = Doncor, Egyptian escort
Horus = Egyptian escort
Sven = Nordic

Argonauts

Jason = Captain, husband to Medea
Heracles = Hercules

Orpheus = Musician, husband to Persephone
Euphemus = Helmsman
Periclymenus = Shape-shifter
Theseus = Athenian hero
Tiphys = Helmsman
Medea = Priestess, wife of Jason
Atalanta = Huntress

Egypt

Akhenaten = Amenhotep IV, pharaoh
Nefertiti = Queen
Meketaten = Princess
Ankhesenpaaten = Princess
Neferneferuaten = Princess
Neferneferure = Princess
Setepenre = Princess
Tutankhaten = Prince
Thutmose = Royal sculptor
Seth = Gem buyer
Panehesy = High priest
Ranefer = General
Nakhtpaaten = Minister

Inland Sea

Ermete = Terramare elder
Bird = Village elder
Arete = Queen of Phaeacia
Alcinous = King of Phaeacia
Aeetes = Colchian king
Apsyrtus = Medea's brother, Colchian captain

Odysseus = Odyssey captain
Minos = Minoan king
Pasiphae = Minoan queen
Asterion = Minoan prince, Minotaur

Mythology

Lorelei = Rhine siren
Lilith = Priestess, queen of Hades
Rhinegold Maidens = Nymphs
Flosshilde = Rhinegold maiden
Alberich = Dwarf, Nibelungen king
Heliades = Trees, seven sisters
Phaethon = Heliades' brother
Hecater = Dark goddess
Circe = Siren
Aphrodite = Siren
Charibdis = Whirlpools
Helios = God of the sun and moon
Symphlegades = Rock spirits
Scylla = Serpent
Haides = God of the underworld
Notus = God of the south wind
Lips = God of the southwest wind
Zeus = God of Olympus
Picus = Woodpecker
Persephone = Goddess of seasons

CPSIA information can be obtained at www.ICGtesting.com
Printed in the USA
BVOW010738231211
278972BV00001B/39/P